The Survivor Stands

Catastrophe Incoming: Volume III

Aimee Donnellan

ISBN (paperback): 978-1-7385843-5-2

ISBN (e-book): 978-1-7385843-6-9

Editor: Quinton Li (https://www.quintonli.com/)

Cover artist: Katelyn McNeely (https://twitter.com/tacticiankate)

Cover typographer: Inorai (https://www.fiverr.com/inorai)

Continuity Expert: Ty Donnellan

www.aimeedonnellan.com

Contents

The Catastrophe Incoming series   V

Content Warnings and Image Descriptions   VI

Fullpage Image   IX

Dramatis Personae   X

Dedication   XI

The Story So Far...   XII

1. Chapter 1   1

2. Chapter 2   12

3. Chapter 3   23

4. Chapter 4   33

5. Chapter 5   44

6. Chapter 6   51

7. Chapter 7 — 59

8. Chapter 8 — 66

9. Chapter 9 — 76

10. Chapter 10 — 92

11. Chapter 11 — 101

12. Chapter 12 — 113

13. Chapter 13 — 125

Afterword — 133

Acknowledgements — 135

Preview — 137

The 'Catastrophe Incoming' Series

1. The Chase Begins

2. The Collection Awakens (October 2023)

3. The Survivor Stands (February 2024)

4. The Labyrinth Beckons (June 2024)

5. *Title to be confirmed* (October 2024)

Books 6-12 to be published in 2025 and onward, exact months to be confirmed.

Content Warnings

This work contains: themes of violence and cruelty, depictions and descriptions of violence and blood, and frequent coarse language. There are also mild sexual references, and violence towards a malevolent being trapped in an animal form.

Image Descriptions

Book Cover

A woman with short orange hair and a flower crown wields a large sword in both hands, poised ready to strike. She wears full armour and an expression of aggressive focus and determination. Behind her, a series of mountains cradles a settlement of buildings with a pillar of smoke rising from them.

The text reads: The Survivor Stands, Catastrophe Incoming: Volume III, Aimee Donnellan

Map of Hanos (following page)

A greyscale map depicting a small town wedged between forests and a mountain range. There is a central area of town with the largest concentration of buildings, with a few more scattered past the main farmlands to the north. Trees are scattered around the area.

Town of Hanos

Dramatis Personae

(IN ORDER OF APPEARANCE)

Wren - *she/her* - a blacksmith's daughter from a farming town, turned warrior, non-mage

Lark - *they/them* - an adventurer and devout follower of the Scholar god, Gifted mage

Reverie - *she/her* - the latest in a line of adventurers who inherit a cursed protector, Disciplined mage

Ferdinand - *he/him* - cursed goose tied to Rosetia family, formerly [REDACTED] [REDACTED] of [REDACTED]

Norak - *he/him* - young guard in the town of Hanos

To everyone who wakes up and chooses kindness every day in a world that sorely needs it: you are the best of us, and I aspire to your heights.

The Story So Far...

While the war against dragons rages across the Theocracy of Izirm, and the Republic of Qelandia, the bishops of the Theocracy are trying to find a way to bring the way to an abrupt end. The adventurer Lark and their friend Wren, are enlisted by a deputy bishop of the Scholar god, Andrian, to help recapture a murderous mage, Nightingale. Lark, who has a complicated history with Nightingale, wrestles with complex feelings as they try to bring her in. They are also distracted by snippets of information on *the Ascension Project*, a secretive endeavour that holds the hope of the Theocracy's future and somehow requires a revered warrior of the Warbringer, Ser Palla, to succeed.

Ultimately, Nightingale's trickery and an impossible decision result in the murderer's escape from Kequm.

Upon using their Wayfinder (a magical teleporter in their possession) to follow her, Lark and Wren find themselves in a magical Collection in the Qelandian mountains. No Nightingale in sight, but malevolent magic ready to strike down everyone inside. They meet Reverie, a musical adventurer and mage (and her horrible companion Ferdinand, a magical goose).

After recruiting Reverie into their murderer catching team and realising that the malevolent magic might be connected to their current mission or the war, they use the Wayfinder to once again try and jump to Nightingale's location. This brings them to a hillside near a small town... where our story continues.

Chapter 1

As a child, Wren had seen a boy in her town being pushed around by others—not bigger or stronger kids, but ones with numbers and jeers that made his pushback futile. Every part of her had screamed to intervene. To do something. But fear froze her in place, and when she broke free of it, she ran home and asked her father what she ought to have done.

"Why didn't you help him?" he had asked.

"I was scared."

"Of course. But you're tough, and think about how that boy would have felt to not be alone. Sometimes, doing nothing is the worst thing you can do. Let me show you how to throw a punch, in case you ever need it."

And so, the next time she had seen the boy being picked on, she jumped into the middle. She and the boy staggered into her home with black eyes and her father was quick to provide everything from laughter to hugs to comforting strawberry tea.

Two things from that day continued to burn through Wren's memory. First, the shock and relief in the boy's eyes when she had leapt into battle for him. Second, the shine of pride in her father's eyes. She had known, with such clarity that she had for nothing else, that she would do anything to keep that pride burning in him. That she could never leave someone without help if she could provide it.

Her father had given Wren everything, and one of the best ways to honour what he had taught was to help those who needed it most. Even if, this time, it meant walking away from home, against his wishes.

You don't need to do this, he had said.

But she did. No matter how often his voice burns in the back of her head, this is what he taught her. Their home had been attacked, and she was the only one with any lead on those responsible. The only one who believes in the clue she found.

It'd been a winding journey of getting caught up in dozens of other adventures, because people needed help and how could she resist? Or because it was so bizarre that she couldn't *not* stick around to see what was going on. But all the while, she has been pushing and prodding for information, to build a trail, and now—

Now, newly arrived by way of magical teleport, Wren stands on a hill. The town below is one she has never seen before, and yet the sight is more familiar to her than anything in the last six months of her life—to say nothing of the last week.

A safe haven. A home. Shrouded in smoke and screams.

The first time Wren saw a town burning like this, with the rage of fire and brutality of ice, it had been her own. No dragon in sight, then or now. Just people—ruining things in that uniquely terrible way that only people can. That day, Wren finally knew fear with intimacy she shares with little else.

Today is different. Today, Wren feels rage. Today, Wren feels *not again, not here, not while I breathe.*

Could it be the same? The same bandits with mages capable of such destruction? Is it more of a coincidence if they are, or if they aren't?

Why has the Wayfinder brought them here? They're supposed to be teleporting toward an erratic, knowledge-hungry murderer.

Wren glances to her side, to where her friends stand. Lark's mismatched eyes dart to different parts of the town below, cataloguing gods-only-know-what details in their remarkable brain. The sun glints off the golden scales on the side of Lark's head as well as the hand they nervously run a hand through their dark hair.

Their gaze flicks across to meet Wren's.

"This is... very not good," they say. "No immediate sign of Nightingale, but either this place has yet another connection to her or she's here. And, there's smoke..."

"You said arson isn't her style," Wren says.

"And in all fairness, was proven wrong about a minute later," Lark counters.

"There isn't just smoke, there's ice." Wren kneels down to dig through her bag for her helmet. She can't stand wearing it but cannot ignore its need if she has the chance to prepare for battle. "She might be here, but someone else is doing this. We need to help, now."

"Definitely," agrees Reverie, their other companion.

A new friend acquired within the last twenty-four hours for her versatile skills with Disciplined magic, Reverie is a walking spectacle of pastel pink skin, teal hair, and golden horns that spiral straight up above her head.

She currently has one hand around the neck of a struggling goose, and the other hand on the reins of her pale gold mare. She walks as if there is nothing odd or difficult about this, but there is tension in her jaw.

Wren cannot hold in the question: "What was he saying to you?"

It is not an ordinary goose. He is something more horrid and remarkable than what Wren is capable of fully comprehending. And he can speak directly into Reverie's head, and vice versa.

"You don't want to know," Reverie says, voice flat. "Let's just say people suffering is his idea of fun, and leave it at that. Anyway!" She smiles, so fast it nearly gives Wren whiplash. "Do you have a plan?"

"Help as many people as possible," Wren says. She begins heading down the hill towards the town, making sure not to slip on the loose dirt on the steep slope.

"Oh. Yeah. Cool," Reverie is quick to say, as she hurries after and somehow manages to all but skip down the slope as if it's easy. "That works. Come on, Melora, good girl."

The mare must trust Reverie an awful lot to follow her down the slope so easily, and she receives copious praise for her trouble.

Wren looks back at Lark, who has been working to get ahead but losing a battle to their uncoordinated limbs. "Does that work for you, Lark?"

She is not usually the one who makes the plans, who takes charge. Even asking the question feels strange.

Lark blinks, perhaps feeling the strangeness of the situation as strongly as she does. They hurry to get to the bottom of the slope onto the main road into the town, one that likely comes from the Grand Highway. Once they are on flat ground, they let out a breath of relief.

"I—yes," they say, fixing their collar. "Obviously. Marvelous. I'm sure Nightingale will reveal herself in due course, if she's here, and if not then that will tell us something too—"

"Good. Now, we need to see how many mages we're dealing with before we get into the town," Wren says.

"Oh! Easy," Reverie says with a grin. "Bird's eye view."

There is an almighty honk as she unceremoniously launches Ferdinand into the air. He catches himself and takes off towards the town, but not before giving Reverie the worst stink eye that Wren has ever seen.

"He's going to report back on numbers, positions, and mages," Reverie says with satisfaction. "That'll help, right?"

"Goose scout," Wren says, eyebrow up. "This week is going to keep getting stranger, isn't it?"

Lark is busy watching the goose disappear over a roof, then turns back to Reverie. "Will the report be... accurate? If I were a spiteful goose, I'd lie."

Reverie smirks. "He has to obey any direct command I give. In this case, a truthful report. So we're good."

"Convenient."

"It's the only part of this thing that is," Reverie says, raising even more questions about the goose than Wren already had.

The trio and the horse creep closer to town, taking it slow and careful until they receive Ferdinand's report. There is no sign of watching eyes as they reach the outskirts, where a wooden wall stretches to form a barrier between the farmland and the centre of town, but that nothing to offset Wren's nerves.

"Just a second," Reverie says, as she spots a secluded alcove where she ties up Melora and promises to check in on her soon. "Don't want her near any fighting, if I can help it."

As they continue on, a pair of townsfolk appear from a side street ahead of them, grimy and panicked. They cast a bewildered look at the new arrivals, and one opens his mouth to speak only to be tugged along by his counterpart, away and out of sight.

"I don't have much experience with bandits," Lark says to Wren. "What sort of organisation might we be looking at? If you have any such experience."

"It really depends," Wren says. "But a town this size would have guards, decent ones. And the bandits still felt confident enough to hit it. The mages probably help with that. They might be bold, and lucky. Or they might be efficient, and deadly."

"So, basically, first point of order is working out which."

"No, first point of order is helping the townspeople, and trying not to die in the process," Wren says. "Any information we get is a bonus."

Lark opens their mouth to speak, then holds her gaze a moment longer, and closes it again. Wren feels a twinge of anxiety—*am I saying too much? Am I giving it away?*—but pushes it aside. Her priorities and experience are sound. And, in this moment, Wren has confirmation that Lark feels the power of their friendship, their support of each other, as complementary and strange and simple as it is. There's no one she trusts more. And yet... it has only been six months, and some things are too hard to say. Some things Wren can barely say to herself.

There are plenty of people smart enough to bring a mage in their bandit group... one would assume. The likelihood of this being *entirely* familiar should be, in Lark's sort of language, astronomical. Right? Her gut isn't so sure. And the worst part about her gut is that she can't ignore it, not for anything. It has led her this far from home already. Where else could it take her?

Miraculously, that is when the goose returns. He lands directly on top of Reverie's head and fluffs his feathers, causing the musician to curse and bat him off.

"Report," Reverie says as she smoothes her hair and glowers at him. "Accurately."

Ferdinand honks at her with defiance before pausing. Reverie nods a few moments later, and gives a half-hearted thanks to her bound protector.

"Ten," Reverie conveys to Lark and Wren. "No mages. At least, not any more. Just warriors, some with mounts. Three look like they're headed out of town."

"And we have two mages," Wren says. "Is your magic helpful in a fight? It's slow, isn't it?" Wren is still getting her head around what different mages of different types can do, but she has observed this much so far, at least.

"It's slow, but it's worth it," Reverie says with a nod. "I could get on a roof and get started. I'd need about a minute from whenever I can see them."

A lot can happen in a minute. Far, far too much. But Wren can stand her ground, especially with Lark's magic backing her up.

"Give it your best," Wren says, as they continue moving deeper into town, past buildings singed or marked with ice. "Whenever we find them."

There is little doubt in her mind about trusting Reverie to have her back. Someone having already saved your life tends to win trust easily.

They have almost reached the thick of it now. A slow approach is safest, to avoid announcing their arrival.

But then a bandit rides into their path.

Wren grips the handle of her blade, but Lark is even faster. Their hand goes to the amulet around their neck—the symbol of the Scholar god, a scroll and quill crossed over each other. With a quick prayer comprised of rapid words and powerful intent, a sheen of golden magic ripples over the bandit's form.

His mouth opens. No sound comes, and his face becomes a powerful red as he tries to bellow louder. Nothing.

Wren strides up and yanks him off his horse. It should not be so easy, but the shock of the magical silence has him unbalanced and pliant. He hits the ground with a thud, and belatedly reaches for his blade.

One kick from Wren's hard boot and the sword goes flying out of his hand. Then, in satisfying rhythm, a well-placed thud of her own sword's pommel at his temple knocks him out cold.

"Nicely done," Lark says, as Wren smacks the horse's rear to send it flying out of town.

"And you."

Reverie laughs. "Wow. You two really have the mage and warrior teamwork down."

"Months of practice," Lark says with a grin. "Now, would you say that roof over there might suit your purposes for magic, Miss Rosetia?"

Reverie follows their gaze. "That'll work, yeah. Are we close enough?"

"If our friend over there is any indicator, I'd say so. Do we need to know anything about your magic?"

Reverie smiles, cocking her head and planting her hands on her hips. "Nah. You'll see it."

With that, she hurries to clamber up some barrels along the house that will get her to the roof. The goose follows her.

"I've never felt so vaguely threatened," Lark says to Wren, making a face.

Wren almost smiles, but she can hear movement down the alley up on their next right, and knows that Lark's estimate was accurate. They creep closer, and Lark's hand finds Wren's shoulder, grasping it as they speak a familiar prayer—their speech is not limited when it is for spells, Wren has realised, perhaps because they are speaking more to the Scholar himself than a person around them.

The magic makes every inch of Wren tingle as it covers her in warm, protective power. A golden sheen covers her skin for a moment before vanishing, but the warmth remains.

Nothing can make anyone completely impervious to harm, or so Lark says, but this spell goes a long way to lessen the piercing of blades or the impact of a hammer. Wren can get right to where she's best.

"Let's go," she says. They peer around a corner and see three bandits down the way. "Alright. Usual front to back?"

Lark does not answer, but they nod and step back.

Wren does not run in. She does not shout a challenge, or rush in with a roar. Why give them the warning? That's ego over strategy. She strides, slow and confident, until one of them spots her and shouts to the others.

Helmets hide their faces, but bewilderment turns their bodies rigid. It lasts only a moment, before one barks at the others to charge her. Wren stops where she is, plants her feet wide and firm, and waits.

You can train your whole life to use a sword, her father had said when they had begun her lessons, *but the greatest thing to sharpen it with is common sense. Wield them together.*

Movement is energy. Energy is precious, especially when outnumbered. No need to move until the last moment. Let them go first and reveal their techniques, their instincts.

She is ready, except that—

There is nothing special about the armour that covers them. But every single one of them has a sash of deep blue tied to their right pauldron. Disbelief catches in her throat, tasting like bile, and for a moment she is not here but home, staring defeat in the face before she has even begun.

Astronomical, she had thought. But her gut, always her gut, right when every part of her wishes so desperately to be wrong. The magic, the chaos, the fear in the eyes of the civilians.

It's the same group. Is it the sheer power of coincidence, or fate? Wren is hardly sure she believes in either. But before her eyes history is repeating. A new town. New victims. And now, even down to this, to Wren standing before too many of them, holding the same sword and determination to stop them.

"Did you sleep in?" the frontmost fighter asks, with a snort. He swings his axe into position. "Stand down, before I cut you down."

"Is that a threat?" Wren asks.

He glances back at his companions, who burst into laughter that rings as horribly familiar as their sashes. "Or a suggestion. Whatever."

Wren lifts her chin, and grips her sword all the tighter. "Noted. And declined."

Chapter 2

How many people get a chance to amend one of their greatest failures? A chance to play it out again, not a rewrite or an erasure but a chance to step up and do better? Wren doesn't know whether to be beyond thankful or if she's going to lose her breakfast to the dirt in front of her.

The one who had issued the warning shifts his weight backward, ready to lunge forward. In a moment he'll be upon her, and the others haven't bothered to move.

Not many people have the nerve to laugh at her these days, but numbers and cruelty can do wonders. While they snicker, memory flashes so vividly and unbidden that for a moment she is somewhere else.

In her town's city hall, facing a group with the same sash, as they turn from their business raiding the vault. Their cackles may not be identical, not down to the person, but the power of the mocking is the same. The same callous disregard for the hurt being inflicted, for the bravery it takes to stand against them.

The first sword is faster than she expects. She isn't ready, and she staggers. The axe swings and meets her sword. Wren does not budge an inch.

Lark isn't in sight, but Wren trusts that they still have her back, just as she trusts that any moment now she will see Reverie's magic come into play.

It is beyond foolish to be standing before them. She is facing death, facing the mercy of those who have already shown they have little, but how can she not? This is her home. This is not her home. But to them, this is just another farm of fodder and coin for the reaping, and she will not let them have it.

The next swing comes and Wren meets it easily. But on her other side she has left an opening and another adversary moves in. His grip shifts on the staff end of his pike before he jabs forward with the thrusting spear end. Wren braces for impact on instinct. There is only a small pressure. Lark's protection, holding strong.

Wren grins while confusion flashes across her attacker's face. He mutters a draconic curse that means something akin to 'fluffy sheep shit bits' (something Wren only knows because her closest neighbour had been a sheep farmer partial to the phrase).

Her greatsword sweeps in front of her, forcing them all back. It's her turn to chuckle now, and it feels so good that she is sure she is lit up bright orange in Lark's vision like a roaring fire.

A week of chasing murderous mages. Trying to understand Theocracy politics. Fighting mysterious magic trying to kill and embarrass anyone it could. Wren has made herself useful for sure, but she has been floundering, grasping at straws of understanding. Hoping that what she thinks or says isn't dense.

To be back on *her* playing field? Sheer relief.

Swing. Block. Another hit that should hurt but barely does. More cursing.

Skill can only go so far. There are too many. The blows come over and over, battering her armour, slipping underneath, sliding across her cheek. Wren chooses her movements carefully. Ducking, weaving, waiting for the right moment and throwing her body into the axe wielder with so much force that her shoulder sends him flying into the brick wall. Their strikes against her are beginning to add up, the stings and aches small but numerous. Wren has held out so much longer than she should have.

The triumph is so close she can taste it. She knocks down the pike wielder, leaving her with only two hesitant longswordsmen.

But then three more emerge from down the way. Making five. Too many when she's already scraped up.

The word 'fuck' sits heavy on Wren's tongue. She cannot release it, cannot show weakness for a moment. It would be too much leverage when she is already unsure she can take them.

Always be realistic about your chances of success, comes more advice from her father. *But never, ever betray any doubt in yourself. The moment they see it, they have you.*

One charges. She blocks, but only by leaving herself open, and the other gets the chance to yank off her helmet and throw it to the ground. He grins and jabs at her exposed right side—

Only to stop short. The bandit's body locks, rigid as stone, other than his eyes that are frantic through the slit of his helmet. His body glistens with golden magic, and Lark's voice fills Wren's ears as they come up behind her, chanting their prayer to maintain the magic.

"Hold this one fast, Scholar, this one who comes to destroy home, to destroy a hearth of knowledge, hold this one fast..."

Wren swings at the one remaining in front of her, taking advantage of the way he keeps glancing sideways at his frozen comrade with obvious fear. It is too easy to kick his knee and get a gash through his piecemeal armour that will keep any sensible person down.

Then, a pommel to the frozen man's head, knocking him out cold.

The approaching three are all that remain. They have slowed their approach, but are still creeping forward.

"Are you sure you wanna do this?" Wren asks them.

One removes her helmet, revealing an older woman with a jagged shortsword and her hair up in a messy grey bun. She sneers at Wren.

Memories slam into Wren like arrows. Piercing. Bombarding. *Wren gets a lucky hit on a woman advancing on her, skimming her eyebrow so that blood begins to trickle into her eye. A cruel shortsword swipes towards her, and Wren cannot move fast enough. It catches her cheek and she cries out as she feels it tear the flesh.* The greatest physical trauma of her life has her touching her cheek with her left hand, feeling the roughness of the scar as she holds the gaze of the woman who had laughed and kicked her to the ground after. Like a strange, twisted mirror, the bandit's hand lifts to her own scar, a fingertip smoothing over line in her eyebrow.

"I should thank you," the bandit says. "It suits me."

Multiple comebacks come to mind. Something about Wren's being bigger. Something about how Wren's makes her look tough too. But the words refuse to come, as if she is Lark and magic has locked her throat. She cannot feign bravado of that kind, pretend to love a scar she is still coming to terms with in her reflection. To take a stand where she has none.

"This feels familiar," the bandit says. "You, barely standing. Me, about to teach you a lesson."

Barely standing. Blood and nausea flows through Wren's head and chest at her words—like sheer will has been keeping them at bay, and the dam breaks the moment she lets herself consider *am I barely standing?*

The street shifts and tilts. Wren blinks until it comes right. Something plays through her ears, a sound she cannot place or fathom. All she can do is shut it out.

The bandits are all but upon her and Lark stops one in their tracks, but the woman and the one on her left keep coming. Wren braces herself as their barrage comes.

Except... it is not a barrage at all. It is a clumsy series of attacks that would easily be put to shame by a skilled twelve year old. The swings are so easy to dodge that Wren has time to halt and stare at the pink magic that is swirling around their helmets like wisps of smoke.

The bizarre periphery sound clarifies itself—Reverie's voice. The distance is too far to make out words, but the tone is harsh and condemning. It has a rhythm that makes Wren shiver, and the magic pulses with deeper colour in time with Reverie's voice, like a drum.

Wren's adversary widens her eyes with terror and realisation. Seeing such a cruel person so powerless for the first time, absolutely shocked by it, is a new and powerful sensation.

"I'm not alone this time," Wren tells her.

The greatsword swings, and the shortsword comes up too slow as if it weighs three times what it ought to, and the bitch goes staggering back. One. Two. Three. She hits the ground, and then her companions follow. It's so easy, it wouldn't be satisfying if Wren didn't know they are such violent scum.

Wren holds position, and waits. No one else comes. Her gaze falls to the unconscious, wounded people at her feet and her mind races to catch up with her heart and body.

It's *them*. Which means it's *him*. It's *now*, and she isn't ready. She has searched and toiled and done everything she can to prepare, but she had never expected to simply walk into this.

A part of her wants to run. Run like she hasn't in years, not since her father taught her a better way. Except that this is the time he would tell her to do just that, to turn and run home, because she cannot be right. She just can't be. So *he* thinks.

Wren stares at her mess of a reflection through the grime and dirt coating her sword. "Sorry, Da," she whispers, unsure if she is talking to the reflection or the parts of her father that reside in her face. "I guess I need to be foolish. If I can be brave enough."

There is a tap on her shoulder and she jumps, blinking at Lark with alarm.

"Don't surprise me when I'm holding the sword," she pleads, horrified at how easily that could have resulted in Lark losing a hand.

"Ah. Sorry." Lark glances down, at their handiwork, then back at her. "Uh. Well done. Here, you're looking a bit unsteady."

Their hand finds her shoulder, and a quick healing prayer steadies the world and relieves the throbbing from Wren's body.

"Thanks," Wren says, with relief.

Lark nods. "Wren, that woman, you and she—"

Wren turns her gaze down as she retrieves her helmet and puts it back in her bag, so that they cannot finish their question. It's unfair; it's necessary, so that she can make it through the next five minutes without her courage dissolving. "Let's get them tied up for the town guard."

Lark makes a small noise, something between a sigh and a whine, and she can see their hands flailing in her peripheral vision. She keeps her eyes away, and vows to apologise to them for it later.

The two of them get to work immediately, and Reverie soon joins them from the roof, with the goose landing on one of the unconscious figures and perching on their upturned rear.

"Wow," Reverie says as she arrives at Wren's side. "That was—holy shit, Wren, you're incredible."

Lark snorts. "What makes shit holy, out of curiosity?"

Reverie blinks, and plants her hands on her hips. "I can't tell if you're joking."

"It's just a peculiar expression."

"I mean, I *guess*, I've never really—" Reverie gestures vaguely in Lark's direction. "You serve the Scholar. Surely if anyone can make shit holy, it's you."

"I'm an academic, a Seeker, not a priest!" Lark sniffs with distaste. "I would argue that nothing can make shit holy. Sometimes shit is just shit."

Wren's hand comes down over her eyes, sweaty and sore from gripping her sword. "Six hours ago, you two were discussing complicated magical theories that sounded totally made up, but weren't. And *this* is what you're on about now?"

They both have the decency to look embarrassed. Wren can only sigh and leave them to their rope work, letting them know she's going to go on ahead and see what she can do.

The square ahead is crowded and half ablaze. Several groups huddle in corners, tending to wounded, while more able people are scrambling for buckets.

Wren hurries in to assist in whatever way she can, only to stop short, having found herself in an abrupt and unexpected acquaintance with a longsword held under her chin.

"You stand alone," its owner growls from her side. "That's the last mistake you'll make."

She's still holding her sword, in case she comes across more of the bandits. Sheer thoughtlessness on her part, in reality, running towards them all as armed and armoured as she is without introducing herself first. Of course they would react like this.

"I'm not with them, I'm here to help," Wren says, as calmly as one can with their jugular under such imminent threat.

The owner of the longsword stands at the same six feet that she does, with orcish blood colouring his skin a lovely shade of dark green. His half plate armour has modest decoration marking him as a town guard. He hesitates at her words and looks her over more carefully, and it is impossible to know what he sees—or perhaps, does not—but he lowers the sword.

"I'm sorry."

"*I'm* sorry," Wren says. She glances at the locals who are now all watching them. "I didn't mean to scare you all. My name is Wren. My friends and I were passing by, saw what was happening... we took out the ones that ran down that way—" She points to the street behind her. "They should be along soon. Let's get this fire out, yeah?"

Fire is hard fought with buckets at any time. With such a start as the one a mage had given it? It's thankless work, but some people with mundane magical control over water rush in to help, and the nearby well allows them to contain the flames to only a few houses.

Harder to fix are the holes blasted through several walls, scorched around the edges.

"There's a street covered in ice," her new friend says. He has stuck close to her, perhaps more out of caution than companionship, but she minds little. "At least that will melt." At last he turns to her and offers a hand. "Norak, by the way."

Wren gives the hand a firm grip. "Wren."

It's about then that Lark and Reverie, both flushed with exertion and collapsing to the ground upon arrival, reach the square with the bandits in tow.

"Wren! Hello!" Lark calls, as if they aren't almost wheezing. "How are things?" They pause and survey the square before she can answer, and their shoulders fall. "Ah."

Green dragons can see, smell and taste emotions. Some kind of full body sense, pure magic, as Lark had explained it. Lark's green dragon eye holds a small measure of that power, but Wren can imagine what it sees now. Swirls of fear and despair, pale yellow and perhaps a very dark blue, if Wren's memory has recalled previous conversations correctly.

"Yeah," Wren says. "But we'll get there. Thanks for bringing them. This is Norak. He's part of the guard here."

"Are you head guard now, if you're the only one who isn't in the infirmary?" a nearby woman asks Norak.

Norak blinks. "I—fuck. I guess so. At least, acting in it."

"The *only* one?" Lark asks with horror.

"Yes, it's been a shit day, if you must know," Norak retorts, rubbing his brow. "And a shit yesterday. Half a dozen guards are alive, but all bedridden with their injuries. So by default, yeah, it's just me. For however long we have left."

His hand shakes where it rests on the sheath of his sword.

"Which will be *ages*!" Reverie chirps as she slides into view. "Hi. Reverie. Good to meet you, Acting Captain Norak." Her voice lowers several notches. "Careful, acting captain. These people are looking at you. Whatever hope they have left rests on you. I know you're freaked, but you can't let them know. You gotta be brave for them. Shoulders back, chin up. Voice steady."

Norak stares at her for a moment, bewildered, and then clears his throat. In time with her instruction, one beat at a time, his posture straightens, he steels his face, and he says: "Yes, of course. Thank you."

"Fantastic," Reverie says, her eyes much more serious than the smile that graces her lips.

"We're here to help, until it's done," Wren tells Norak.

He keeps his face composed while his eyes flash with relief. "Then let's get them to the guardhouse."

Chapter 3

The guardhouse is deserted. Not like old history, but like a story left unfinished, a book half-filled, with nibbled snacks and cups on desks and papers all over the reception.

Norak stares at it all. His jaw tightens. "In here," he says, making a turn with his half of the prisoners. Wren follows with her half and they get them into the two cells that this small guardhouse has.

There is no question of their affiliation. Each one has the same sash, in the same place.

Wren's adversary is beginning to stir. She's unarmed, probably not a threat, but Wren takes a step back and closes the cell door to be safe.

"What's your name?" Wren cannot help but ask. They have crossed blades twice, marked each other, lived to see each other again. There's no real warrior code, not one that anyone is forced to follow, but it seems wrong that they do not know each other. Names hold power and respect, after all.

The woman narrows her eyes. "Darla."

"Wren. But, maybe you already knew that."

Darla sniffs. She gives no indication one way or another. There is only contempt.

"How long until the next attack?" Wren asks. "Or are you done?"

"We let you live," Darla says. "You get in our way again—"

"Not the best threat when you've already tried and failed," Wren retorts. "It's not *you* I'm worried about now. It's the others. Next attack?"

Darla spits on the ground near Wren's feet. "We didn't get this far by running our mouths. Run, or stay and die."

Wren wants to ask about her leaders. Her knuckles are white where they grip the cell bars, and she startles when a hand lands on her hand. She knows it is Lark before she looks.

"Wren," they say, their brown eye soft as it regards her. "Why don't you tell us what's going on?"

Norak makes coffee, and they all gather around Norak's desk. He curtly disagrees with the suggestion to use the captain's office, and no one pushes the matter further. Wren stands freely, clutching her cup with both hands, while Reverie perches on another desk nearby and Lark makes mockery of the act of sitting with the way they drape their legs over the spare chair's arms.

"They hit my town about a year ago," Wren says. "We had guards, like here, but you can't—"

"No guard is prepared for that kind of magic," Norak says, and Wren nods.

"I should have gone home," she continues, staring into her cup. "Should have looked after my family. That's the whole reason I learned how to use Da's sword. But I saw them at the town hall. About to take the vault, take everything that would help fix what they were destroying. And I just—"

Wren stops and sips at the coffee. It is hot enough to burn her tongue, and she swallows through the pain.

"Da taught me to help, not to run." She says it more to herself than them, the joined scenarios playing over in her head until they blur.

Lark's eyes haven't left her, and when she meets them, the shine of them and the intensity of their gaze makes her heart stutter.

"...Wren, how many were there?"

"Half a dozen or so," Wren says, pressing her lips together. "Didn't stand a chance."

"But you're alive," Norak breathes, shaking his head. "You raised a blade to them and lived. How did you get away?"

"I didn't. They just... left me." Wren rubs her temple. "I woke up and they were gone. And then, to be even more boneheaded... I went after them."

"Wren," Lark says with horror.

"I know." Wren closes her eyes, swallows hard against the lump in her throat. "I followed their tracks, and that's when I saw a cufflink in the dirt. I'd never paid attention to a cufflink in my life, but this one—this one I knew."

Wren has never had the attention of so many people for so long. Three sets of eyes watching her. Reverie is more silent than Wren had yet to know her, a rapt audience in herself with one hand perfectly clasped over her mouth. "But then I passed out. I was too injured. I'd lost too much blood. I woke up in my bed. My father and brothers had found me, gotten me home. And when I went back to look for it, the cufflink was gone."

"Did it belong to that man from the illusions? In the Collection?" Reverie asks.

They had all been tormented, in the Collection. Some entity toying with them, finding their deepest weaknesses and giving them face and voice, letting everything cut deep. Wren's, of course, had been her greatest uncertainty: her greatest enemy, or her greatest error.

And naturally, Reverie had managed to put that together in an instant.

"My uncle has a pair of cufflinks made of good silver, in the shape of lily flowers," Wren says, swallowing hard. "They were a gift from his husband. And I saw one of them in the dirt that day. He and his mercenary band were supposed to be far, far out of town. And none of it made sense, he's a mercenary and not a bandit, and he doesn't have any mages like the ones that hit us, but I just—"

There is a pregnant pause as she stops, and they stare.

"Why else would they leave me alive?" Wren throws her hands up and her coffee flies all over her. With only a curse under her breath, she wipes her face with her hand. "If they knew they might get in trouble for killing me. If the cufflink was there, before it got buried in the mud."

"The illusion. Your uncle. It taunted you for being uncertain," Lark says, with a tilt of their head. "Are you? Is this just a theory?"

Wren is so caught in their words, their face, that she is startled by Reverie handing her a cloth which she's fetched from another room.

"Yeah," Wren is forced to admit. "Da, he told me to let it go. Said it was impossible. It's his brother, I get it, it's the last thing he wants to believe. But I can't help it. I just—"

"You feel it," Reverie says from beside her, voice soft. "You know?"

"Yeah," Wren breathes, wetting her lips with her tongue. "I... I think so. It won't let me go."

"And this gut feeling that won't let you go, it's that your uncle is behind all of this," Norak says.

"Yeah." Wren sighs and shakes her head. "But I don't even know how that would help, if I was right. He hit his old home, his family's home. He left it standing but... he still killed and hurt and stole. So he's no family of mine anymore, is he? I doubt I'll get his mercy twice."

"Probably not," Norak agrees. "But it does mean we can know our enemy. What else can you tell me about him?"

Wren swallows. It's a mess of a thing, useful information entwined with personal memories that ache and sting just at the thought.

"He's been a mercenary leader for a long time. Several decades. His husband is his partner in it—they built up the company together." Her uncles. The model couple in her life growing up. Two perfect opposites, Vasil's steady calm and smiles to her uncle's fiery laughter and enthusiasm. They had helped her improve with her sword, given her tips that only people who have seen countless skirmishes could offer. "Their armour is identical, full plate with a helmet. Two blades crossed on the breastplate, one much larger than the other. One for each of them—my uncle uses a two-handed blade like me, his husband Vasil favours having a weapon in each hand—and then the blue sash like you've seen on their people."

Wren runs through a few other things, some stories of the grand successes the pair of them would spin, trying to pull the tactics out of them but finding that her brain feels slow. It's struggling to wade through the emotions that have flooded her.

"Thank you," Norak says, seeming satisfied. "So his husband is Vasil. What's your uncle's name? With their different temperaments, we'll want to know which one we're dealing with."

"... Viken," Wren says, through a lump in her throat. She's been avoiding even thinking the name for so long. But she can't do that anymore. "He looks a decent bit like me. Human, ginger but starting to grey a bit. Tall and broad. Vasil's part elven, dark skin, just as big as Viken. No bright elven colours." Nothing like whatever Reverie's got going on. She might be Demonblood, but Wren will wager that there's at least one strong elven line in her family's history, coloured pink and teal and gold as she is.

"I'll get the word out," Norak says. Wren can't help but think that if the townsfolk are close enough to spot Viken or Vasil by description, it will probably be too late. But at least they'll know to run for their lives. "We'll also need scouts, so that we know when they mobilise."

For Lark or Reverie to be quiet individually is remarkable—for them to manage it simultaneously ought to be impossible. But they have both just been sitting, listening, waiting.

Wren looks at Lark, to ensure they can speak now that it's fitting for them to do so.

"So, your uncles might be attacking this town, and somewhere among all of that is Nightingale. Wonderful." Lark says it, of course, like it is the exact opposite.

"Maybe they'll take each other out," Reverie says, brightly, only for both Lark and Wren to wince. "I mean, not—oh shut up." The last part is directed at the goose, who she smacks over the head while he cackles.

"We'll deal with Nightingale when she appears, or we'll find her after the town is safe," Wren says.

Lark's knee is bouncing so violently it is in danger of detaching from their lanky leg. "Yes. I suppose that's the only sensible course of action."

"Who's this Nightingale person?" Norak asks.

"A murderer we're following," Lark says. "Pray to whatever god you choose that she is *not* in Hanos. For everyone's sake."

Norak blinks, then mutters a prayer to the Life Giver with his hand over his heart. A moment later, he looks up. "So… we were thinking of surrendering, since they claim to only kill those who raise arms against them. As beaten down as we are, the best way to keep the people safe is by not doing so."

"We have no idea if they'll honour that," Wren says.

"They have, so far." Norak frowns. "Well, at least, they killed three yesterday. The guards that came to meet them, that stood against them first. That's when they laid down the rule, but everyone else managed to get away injured—except for the librarian, of all people, we found her dead over her desk when we did a sweep of the town."

"The librarian?" Lark asks, rather sharply.

"Yes," Norak says with sorrow. "Such a wonderful lady, so committed to her work. I can't see her fighting them at all, it makes no sense." He sighs. "Anyway, other than that it's held true or close to it, and if I'm acting captain, if the people's safety falls to me—"

"And without us, surrender would be the right call." Wren holds his gaze. "But they will take everything this town has to give, and that will make rebuilding the worst burden a town of injured, grieving people could imagine. I've seen it. Lived it. With us here, you have a chance to protect what you have left. With the right plan, scouts might be able to find where they've taken the town's gold. With the right plan, someone might even be able to bring some of it back."

Norak' eyes shine with something, something bright but tentative as his gaze moves between all three of them. Wren desperately hopes that she is right in thinking they can do this, that she isn't weaving a tale of competence she cannot live up to. She *is* better now. She has powerful friends with her. But is it enough?

Wren needs to find Viken. Needs to look him in the eye, and finally confront him about what he did to her home. But the thought of it makes her feel sick, makes her want to run and hide, want to plead to the Battle Maiden or whoever will hear her, *I'm not ready, even just a few more days, please*. But, then, perhaps that is never how life works. Life doesn't wait for you to be ready.

Oblivious to her struggle, Norak nods as he looks around them all, and smiles. "Okay. With you all here? We could do that. You're right, if there's a chance we can get our gold back, we need it. But I'll need your guarantee, that you'll do everything you can to protect the people here. We'll be taking a risk, and any lost lives will be on all of our heads."

It's a sobering thought, hard to swallow, and it's an odd moment of Wren looking between Reverie and Norak who seem to be struggling with it also.

Lark, meanwhile, simply nods at Norak. "I'm a healer. I can make immediate rounds to tend to your wounded, and keep them alive in the next skirmish. We're with you."

"Thank you." Norak stands and offers a hand out for Lark to shake, and then Wren. "We are so, so fortunate that you're here. The gods have smiled on us today."

Wren grips his hand and gives a small smile, with an exhale that is too fast. What can she say to that? When hope comes back to someone's eyes after being nearly snuffed out? When you're not the hero you may look like?

"Just glad we could help."

"I'd like to investigate the librarian's death, when possible," Lark says. "The timing is incredibly suspicious, given who might have arrived in town yesterday."

Lark has a point. A librarian, someone by nature full of knowledge, is exactly the kind of prey Nightingale would seek out.

"If Norak hasn't seen her, then it doesn't seem like she's still here," Wren says. "Which means she can wait. We have to make sure the town is safe first."

Lark purses their lips, and she can see their conflicting priorities battling through their different, fidgeting limbs. "Yes. Of course."

Norak looks between them. "What's our first move, do you think? Should we try interrogating them again?"

Wren shakes her head. "They're too loyal. We won't get anything from them, not without methods we don't want to use. I say for now, let's post a guard on them, and work on barricades. We need to be ready for the worst."

Chapter 4

THEY SPLIT INTO PAIRS. Lark and Reverie head to the town hall (after a Melora check-in), which has become a mass infirmary, to heal everyone they can with their magic. If they finish early, they're going to check for trickier town entrances the bandits might be able to use to sneak past the barricades.

Wren and Norak, meanwhile, are busy locating and hauling every bit of timber in town they can find that isn't needed to keep a building standing. It is the most peaceful few hours Wren has passed in a while.

In theory.

The problem with manual labour is that it leaves the mind too open to wandering, right into the territory that Wren needs to not be lingering on.

"You're not a guard," Norak says, as they load timber into a cart, and she's so grateful for a chance to talk and not be in her own head that she nearly cries.

"...nope," Wren replies, and has to wonder where he's going with this.

"But you fight better than if you'd trained as one."

"You haven't seen me fight, yet."

"Well, you must, or you wouldn't have beaten so many of them."

Wren snorts. "I beat so many of them because I had two mages backing me up. I *am* good, but not a one woman army."

"Who trained you?"

"My father, mostly." Wren smiles, until she doesn't, until it falls from her face like a stone. "And sometimes, my uncles. They were far more skilled, gave me challenges that were so much *more*. But in recent years, they were away. And now I know why."

Norak nods. "I'm sorry, Wren."

"Me too."

"So what does your father do?"

"He's a smith. He just thinks there's merit to knowing how to use the weapons you make."

"Smart man. So you're a blacksmith's daughter who isn't a guard, and you're here instead of home. So what is it, exactly, that you do?" Norak asks.

Wren thinks it over. Imagines the face he'd make if she explained the week she's had, if he didn't simply laugh and assume it was all made up.

"I suppose I just... gave myself the job of being Lark's bodyguard. They have the self-preservation skills of a baby bird, and I thought the travel could help me find my uncle."

Norak hums with understanding. "So, it's revenge, then?"

Wren makes a face. She has never discussed this with anyone. There might be safety in confiding in a near stranger, but the spoken reality feels awful just to weigh on her tongue, let alone consider releasing.

I don't know if I can take the revenge I'm seeking, and if I do I don't know if I'll forgive myself for it.

"We'll see," she says instead. "What about you? How long have you been a guard here?"

"Since I turned eighteen," Norak says, with a boyish, tusky grin that takes five years from his already youthful face. "Bit of a family tradition since my mum's side moved here from Kanin a few generations back."

It's a lovely sentiment, until Wren remembers something he had said at the start. "Wait, but you said the other guards were all—"

"Yeah, my mother's in the infirmary," Norak says, and he laughs but it catches in his throat. "Last I heard she's been trying to threaten people into letting her leave. But she took a sword to the side. She can't even stand, she'll tear the stitches."

"I'm sorry," Wren murmurs.

"She always told me that armour stops you from being able to fight properly, that it gets in the way," Norak says, shaking his head. "I guess it's a cultural thing, in the nomadic tribes. But I would argue that a sword in the side *also* gets in the way of fighting properly, so I'll take armour. She might be my mother, but I need to do things my way, not someone else's way. Not even hers."

Hard logic to fault. Wren can appreciate that some people take speed and mobility over metallic protection, but truly could never picture walking into a fight so vulnerable to sharp objects.

"Fair enough," Wren says. "If you know what your way is. I'm... not sure I do."

"I think everyone knows what their way is. Deep down. It's in your gut, your heart. You know what's *you* and what isn't."

He sounds so sure. Wren looks away and mumbles an agreement, hating how the insincerity sits in her stomach. But if she thinks on it any longer, it will turn to envy, and that would be an absurd thing to carry today.

"You sound like my da," Wren says instead of anything else, and it is truly the highest compliment she could pay anyone.

Norak grins, and they push the cart forward and begin on the next load of lumber.

It's hot work, especially in the armour, but after their last conversation and the current danger, no mention of removing their plate sets is ever voiced. They're far too tricky to get back on in a hurry if a surprise attack were to appear.

"So if you left home after the attack... what were you doing before? You were already training. You must have wanted adventure."

Adventure. A thing from stories, a thing for other people. A fancy, a fantasy. Not ever something for her to seek out. It had, however, decided that it cared little for her plans and that it was going to seize her with both hands and throw her headfirst into a reckless Seeker's path.

It's looking back through a morning mist, trying to remember life before the attack, trying to remember how she had seen the world and her place in it.

"I think I wanted to run a flower shop, actually," Wren says. An odd smile pulls on her lips as she thinks on it. "My specialty is flower crowns. I think that's what I wanted. I trained because my father wanted to pass on his skills, and my brothers weren't interested in taking up the sword. I was happy doing that while I figured everything out. Swordplay, smithing, it was all just skills but never *me*."

"Selling flowers." Norak hoists a small dining table onto his shoulders, and grins. "I love that. A woman of vision."

"So I was realising," Wren says. "I could only figure so many big things out at a time."

"Sure," Norak says cheerfully. "And that theoretical flower shop isn't going anywhere, and neither is home. They'll be ready when you are—" He stops dead, smile falling and eyes flicking around the street of half-ruined houses. "Or... so we always think, I guess. I was worried about *dragons*, and here we are. No dragons. Just dickheads."

"Yeah, I could really do without dragons on top of everything else," Wren says. "One flew over us a few days ago, in Kequm. I nearly shat myself."

Norak stops in his tracks. "In Kequm? What?"

Wren does some quick math and realises his bafflement. "Oh. Uh. Magic transport. Teleport. Lark has a thing."

"Okay, sure," Norak says, with a necessary dismissiveness that she understands deep within her soul, because when someone says something so absurd that relates to magic you've never seen, there is no other possible way to react. "But... a dragon flew over? I didn't hear anything about that. But. I guess I wouldn't, if it was so recent."

He's right. The news could have never made it to him yet, without magic being involved. The general war correspondence isn't exactly speedy or reliable.

"As far as I know, no one was hurt," Wren says, shrugging. "It didn't attack, even though the wards were down. It just roared and flew over."

"Why wouldn't it attack?" Norak asks. "It's war. That's an easy flyby on what has to be their highest priority target."

"Maybe they didn't want to hurt civilians," Wren says, before catching herself and frowning. "Except, I guess they didn't care about that in the opening attack. The declaration. Unless it was a dragon that is completely neutral, isn't part of their front."

"A dragon civilian, you mean?" Norak says it incredulously, but tilts his head. "I guess if we have them, they would."

"But if you're a dragon civilian, why do it at all?" Wren asks.

The more she thinks on it, the less sense it all makes and the more her stress headache grows. This line of inquiry feels important, but it is simply too much when piled on top of the current situation.

Norak pats her on the shoulder. "Today, let's worry about bandits," he says, perhaps suffering from a similar headache.

They keep loading their cart and get it to one of the town entrances where some of the townsfolk have begun the barricade work and are grateful for the materials. Once unloaded, Wren and Norak keep moving.

They've been at it about two hours when they run into Lark and Reverie, who are coming up another street, looking satisfied but tired.

"Wren!" Lark calls, waving as they jog up. "How's it all going?"

"Alright so far," Wren says. "What about you two?"

"Word got around fast about my healing, so we had to triage a bit," Lark says with a smile. "I had to preserve some of my energy in case of bandits later, but no one will be dying of infection or blood loss, or suffering from extreme pain. That's a good start."

Norak releases a long breath. "How's the orcish lady who got impaled? Goes by Latia?"

"Oh, wonderful lady, she tried to recommend me upper body strength routines," Lark says with delight. "I see the resemblance, now."

Wren has to smother a giggle at the idea of Lark attempting pushups. "Did she try to convince you she's battle ready?"

"She did, so I jabbed her in the side to prove her wrong," Lark says mildly. "She sat down rather quickly after that. I don't know if I made an enemy or won her eternal respect."

"She has that confusing impression on people," Norak says. "Sounds like you handled her well."

"Sounds like my grandmother," Reverie mutters. "Minus the respect."

"Fascinating, I have questions," Lark says to her, immediately.

"That's nice for you," she replies, just as fast, and with a pleasant smile that seems about as sincere as a carnivorous plant asking for a hug.

"We are in your debt, Lark," Norak says with a shake of his head. "Truly."

Lark mimics the action, but in disagreement instead of disbelief. "No. When the ability to help sits so readily in your hands, to not do so is nothing short of negligent. My magic is a gift, not to be hoarded but passed on to others."

Which is why Lark and Wren had clicked immediately, isn't it? It's her father's philosophy, in the hands of someone utterly different, with the same idea of the duty they all have to one another. A duty of solidarity, of kindness, of action where it is demanded.

And yet, Lark remains a fascination. They can say these things, help and help until they are utterly spent but act as though it is as easy as breathing. Then, on days like the ones in Kequm this week, everything falls away when they are faced with someone they love spouting a different ideal. That call to action, frozen, their perspective and priorities so twisted that Wren has to reach out and check that they are still by her side at all.

Nightingale is dangerous because of her magic. Her murderous intent. Her unknown goals and allies. Her lack of care for anyone but herself and perhaps Lark. But most of all, and least apparently, she is dangerous for the influence she has over Lark. And Wren is not sure how readily anyone else knows this.

She makes a note to mention it to Reverie, if they get a moment alone before they find the awful redhead. If they're to survive Nightingale, Reverie needs to know about their greatest weak spot.

"I did a bit of healing too, but mostly people wanted me to sing," Reverie is saying to Norak when Wren tunes back into the conversation. "I'm from Cythos so we have a lot of the same old favourites."

"Your singing *was* splendid, you really do have a wonderful voice," Lark says to Reverie with a broad smile.

The demonblood musician flushes a darker shade of pink in her cheeks, highlighting her freckles further. "Thanks, Lark."

Wren, randomly, finds herself wondering how powerful she might feel if she were able to make Reverie blush like that herself. It's such a peculiar intrusion that she's tempted to smack herself in the face to clear it out, if it wouldn't make her look absurd.

"Anytime, Rosetia," Lark says, only to add, "by which I mean, only when you least expect it." They clap their hands together and look back to Wren and Norak. "So, what next?"

"Well, we'll keep working on the barricades. Did you have time to scope out the other entrances?" Wren asks.

"Ah. Not yet."

"Then that's a good start."

Reverie grins. "Yes ma'am."

Hearing *ma'am* gives Wren hives in an instant. "Don't call me ma'am, unless you wanna be Miss Rosetia."

Reverie tilts her head, eyebrow quirking for a moment before a frown settles over it. "Yeah. Okay. No."

Wren nods, glad they understand each other somehow. She has no idea what to make of the fact that Reverie seems to enjoy her last name coming from Lark, *or* that she does not want it from Wren. Reverie has flirted blatantly with them both in the singular day of their acquaintance so far.

This is exactly why Wren has never found the time or energy to pursue romance. It's far too complicated and distracting.

Norak, thank the gods, clears his throat and brings her back to reality. "So. On with it, then?"

Wren nods. "See you later, you two," she says to Lark and Reverie, and they part ways once again.

"Are you alright?" Norak asks as they walk away. "You seem like you have a lot on your mind."

"If I told you about the week I've had, you wouldn't believe me," Wren promises. "The dragon was one of the easiest parts. I can only keep up with so much, you know?"

"... okay, I'll believe you that I wouldn't believe you," Norak says, with a small laugh. "Let's move stuff. Keep it busy and simple."

"It's so nice being around someone normal," Wren says with relief.

"I bet."

They work for another hour in comfortable silence, until they are ready to transport their current load to the eastern town entrance. They've just gotten a grip on one handle of the cart each when there is an awful crash from the north, followed by screams.

"Shit," Norak says, as they drop the cart in unison and break into sprints towards the commotion.

It's only a few streets away, and they know it the moment they see it—a building frozen solid has now fractured and collapsed. A crowd is gathered around the edge of the rubble.

"Gods," Wren murmurs. She had never thought she would consider her own town lucky, but their buildings had not suffered such damage from the mages.

This is a nightmare. Wood frozen so solid it's a block of ice born anew, slanting angles of bright and glistening white. The strongest of the townsfolk are trying to shift it and wincing at the burn of the cold from their hands.

But the worst part? Screams from inside.

Chapter 5

THE SCREAMS COULD BE pain or terror or both. It is impossible to tell, but Wren's feet drag her forward before her brain can comprehend how to react.

"Back!" she says, quietly at first and then louder for everyone to hear. "Back! It might shift again."

As she waves her hands, the bystanders part and withdraw, leaving a path for her to move forward and examine the icy deathtrap of a structure.

"There's still two inside," someone says, from behind her.

Fuck.

There are three gaps she might fit through. Only one is likely to be safe from debris if any other sections collapse. There isn't time to check, only to decide if she is taking the risk or not.

Two inside. How can she not?

Wren takes a deep breath and ducks under the icy beams. It's dark, with scattered rays of light from the gaps in debris above.

Two inside there might be, but Wren cannot make them out and must move further in.

"Who's stuck in here?" Wren asks, not too loud, just enough to be heard. "I'm coming to get you."

There is a pause. Then comes a small voice. "We're over here. My dad, my dad is stuck. I can't lift it. It's too heavy."

"It won't be for me," Wren promises. There's every possibility that it's not true at all, but none of them can afford for that to be the case, so she's staking everything in optimism and sheer belief. She walks in a crouched position to avoid touching the fallen ceiling, but with her arm up ready to catch it if it gives out. "Stay where you are. Nice and still."

"... okay."

A bit further in, and Wren sees them. Covered in a sprinkle of icicles, a child with curls of dark hair gripping the hand of a larger figure. He's sprawled on his stomach, shattered bits of frozen wood covering his back, including a larger beam keeping him down.

"Is he awake?" Wren asks.

The child shakes her head.

Wren smiles, to try and reassure her. "What's your name?"

"Peony."

Wren's smile widens, now even more genuine. "I like peonies."

Peony smiles back, with a glimmer of hope that Wren swears to preserve at all costs. "Can you help my dad?"

"I'm gonna do my best." Wren comes to crouch next to them. Piece by piece, slow as anything and praying to the Maiden and the Winter Wolf and the Life Giver with every spare thought she has, she shifts the smaller bits of wood from the man's back until the beam is all that remains.

A crack above them has Wren nearly jumping out of her skin. It is a needed but awful reminder that the rest of the ceiling will be coming down soon.

"Shuffle this way, Peony," Wren whispers, so that she can set her legs wide and lift the beam with one arm while her other pulls Peony's father free from his trap.

Her fingertips scream from the cold. But he is free, and now the three of them simply have to escape in time. (Simply, as if it is anything close.) Wren gets the man settled over her shoulder, the weight of him significant but manageable, and takes Peony's hand.

"Let's move," Wren says to the girl.

They've made it halfway when there is another crack above them, louder than before, and a grinding of friction that evaporates too quickly to mean anything but—

"Peony, run! Run for the outside!"

The girl, thank the gods, bolts for the shine of daylight. Her hand leaves Wren's in the exact moment that Wren must bring up her whole right hand, to twist her body to catch the falling ceiling.

Her knees almost buckle from the weight of the frozen wood as it thuds against her armour. Metal plates dig into Wren's body where they shouldn't. Bruises will come later, of that she is sure.

One arm holding the ceiling, which she cannot allow to fall on the person she is carrying with her other arm. She may not have much maneuverability, but she has even less time before her strength fails her and they're both crushed to death. Wren cannot let her strength fail her now, today of all days.

One foot sliding forward in the dirt. One arm taking the ceiling at a time so she can shift her body a foot closer to the exit. Her shoulders are taking it all. Repeat. Repeat. Over and over, closer and closer.

Wren's body begins to shake from the exertion, but they are so close now. It's almost over.

"Wren!" As soon as Norak can see her through the gap, he dives through it to take the last of the weight of the wood, so that she can make it the last eight feet and get her charge to safety.

"Dad!" comes the immediate cry of Peony.

Wren lets her knees give out on her, meeting the dirt with gratitude and gently lying Peony's father on the ground. His chest still rises and falls with breath.

Success. For now.

"He needs a healer," Wren says to the people around. "My friend can help, if someone can get them. I just... need a minute."

The building collapses behind her as Norak stumbles out from the edge with the help of another young man.

"The dragonblood healer," Norak says to those around. "Someone find—"

"I'm here!" Lark calls out. "We came as soon as we heard, we just—"

They stop short at the sight of Wren in the dirt. If she looks half as bad as she feels, it would explain the expression of horror on their face.

"Wren, I leave you alone for *ten minutes*—"

Wren has to laugh. "That's usually my line. I'm just sore. Look at him first, please."

Lark swallows, surveys the situation, and is quick to do exactly that. Meanwhile, on their heels is Reverie, who takes the chance to kneel in front of Wren instead.

"Are you trying to fight impossible battles again?" Reverie asks, half flirt and half fond.

It *is* an uncanny similarity to yesterday, when she had to stop Wren from trying to slice through magical branches that kept growing back no matter how many cuts they took.

"No," Wren says. "Just a ceiling."

Reverie's lips spread in a grin. "Checks out. You've got some scrapes, again. Want me to fix them?"

"Didn't we just do this?"

"Well, if we end up here again tomorrow, then I'll think you're doing it on purpose."

Wren fights a blush, but her cheeks are probably already ruddy with cold and exertion, so perhaps it's pointless. She means to answer, with something deflective, but nothing comes out.

Reverie's smile is too knowing. She does, however, diligently begin patching up Wren's small wounds on her cheeks and hand. The rhythm and sweetness of Reverie's voice is soothing, fueling the ebb and flow of soft pink magic across Wren's skin.

I am not getting this flustered by a pretty girl holding my hand, Wren tries to tell herself. It's bullshit. But then, *pretty girl* is a drastic understatement for a woman as beautiful as Reverie.

Luckily, Lark manages to come in and shatter the moment by swooping in and asking several exasperated versions of *what in the world were you thinking*. Of course, Lark is quite adorable when they're fretting, so that's a whole other problem.

Wren decides there is no answer that will satisfy anyone involved, and simply gets to her feet so she can brush the ice shards off her armour.

"Let's get back to barricade building," Wren says, as if her arms don't ache from the mere thought.

A commotion murmurs through the crowd as an old man bursts through his fellow townsfolk. He shouts a name that Wren doesn't recognise, but runs to the man Wren had saved.

Peony is immediately pulled into a hug by the new arrival.

"I came as soon as I heard," he says. "They said you were trapped, that they weren't sure if—"

"We were rescued, Pa," Peony tells the man who must be her grandfather. "That woman there, she got us out."

She points to Wren, who freezes, caught in the gaze of his teary eyes. He gets to his feet with a wince and crosses to her at once.

"Thank you," he says, reaching for her hand and gripping it tight. "*Thank you*. My family, my whole life, you saved them. I can never repay you, but if there is anything at all—"

"No, nothing," Wren says, too fast, taken aback. "Seeing you all together is enough."

"You held up a *building*," Peony says with an awed shake of her head. "I bet someone will write a song about you one day."

Wren tries to laugh in a dismissive way. It comes out like a choked sound. "I doubt it."

The goose, Ferdinand, honks from Reverie's side. It sounds eerily close to laughter, which is probably why Reverie kicks him. The honking persists regardless.

"You risked your own life to save strangers," the old man says, still trying to make some kind of point.

Wren's ears burn from having so many eyes on her at once, dozens of people with various degrees of admiration and curiosity. Her stomach twists and all she knows is that she needs to get away. Now. She certainly doesn't need to be thinking of how recklessly she had acted.

"It doesn't matter. I mean—I'm glad you're all okay," Wren says. "But if we don't get back to work preparing for the next attack, there will be nothing left to write songs about."

With that, perhaps the most cynical and short thing she has ever uttered, Wren turns and begins walking away. Her heart pounds in her chest like she's running for her life, more fearful than when she had been moments from being crushed.

Wrong. Wrong wrong wrong.

Chapter 6

To be looked at and talked about like some great hero of songs? It's unprecedented. Wren has helped people before, but Lark and their magic tend to consume most attention. She has never given it any thought, too pleased at an outcome where regular people come out safe and happy.

Being at the centre of that attention, as a mere concept, never crossed her imagination, let alone how it might *feel*.

It feels like a stone in her chest. It's hypocrisy, heavy against her heart. Her most firm ideal is of killing being a final resort, that no one outside the law should have the right to impart such finality on another. And yet, her plans for her uncle go against it.

Hypocrite. Liar.
But there's no easy answer.

Waking up every day, so at war with herself, is taking its toll. Today everything is hitting so much harder, each praise hammering right into her heart.

You can't even agree with yourself. How can you stand for anything?

Assuming to know best would be worse.

In a simple world, her uncle would be deserving of death, or not. Guilty and too much of a danger, or worthy of mercy. She would give anything to not be the one to decide, but with the war raging the authorities of Qelandia are simply too far away and too busy. The council cannot prioritise one band of bandits over all else.

Selfish vigilante.

But there's no one else.

Who is going to hold him accountable, if not someone who is both a victim and a relation? It might be something close to patricide, but it might be necessary.

A hero would know the right thing to do, and could commit to it wholeheartedly. Wren knows she is no hero, because nausea rages within her gut like a sea in a storm, battering waves that rise and fall with violence.

Weak.

But I'm trying.

Behind her is noise. It's an annoyance that only makes her walk faster. Away, away, away.

"Wren!"

Her name. Reverie's voice. Not worry, not quite. Uncertainty.

Wren stops, abruptly, and feels Lark's wiry form collide with her back. Then comes a yelp and a thud on the ground. There is more amused goose honking, and Wren turns to Lark lying in the dirt, sighing at the clouds.

"Is that to be the sound I hear every time I encounter misfortune?" they lament.

"Yeah, he sucks like that," Reverie says. "Ferdinand, shut the fuck up."

The goose quiets, and glares, which is a thing that until now Wren had thought geese could not do. Stare menacingly, sure, but glare? What an extraordinary, horrid creature.

Wren offers a hand to Lark, without saying a word. They take it and get to their feet.

"What's wrong?" they ask as soon as they're vertical again.

"Nothing," Wren lies.

Lark sighs, with worse exasperation than they had shown to the clouds. "Wren. I can see these things, you know. You're covered in grey and blue."

"And what does that mean?"

"It means you're upset, and uncertain. Which is understandable, with everything going on here, but please. Let me help. I've never—" Lark stops. Swallows. "I've never heard you talk to anyone like that."

Wren squares her jaw. "I know. I didn't mean to."

"I believe you."

Wren glances at Reverie, who has been uncharacteristically silent. Her eyes are fixed on Wren, intense and analysing, and something about it makes Wren feel far more exposed than knowing Lark can see her base emotions.

"Wren's a big girl, I'm sure she's fine," Reverie says a moment after Wren meets her gaze. "And she's right, we have stuff to do, or we're all fucked. I'm too pretty to die in the middle of nowhere. So let's go. You can flap around her later."

Lark whirls around in a flurry of brown coat. "I do not *flap*, Rosetia—"

And just like that, the two of them are off again, arguing over utterly nothing, and Wren can only wonder if Reverie had baited Lark deliberately. Unable to shake the feeling that Reverie has just covered for her on guesswork alone, Wren feels gratitude wash through her system and calm every part of her body that had been battling fight-or-flight.

It is too easy to chuckle at the verbal sparring between her companions, and to wonder how adamantly Lark would deny enjoying it.

The trio walk as two of them bicker and one listens. They pass children drawing on the cobbles with coloured chalk, a small gaggle of them that are enthusiastically giggling and squealing as they switch colours between them.

"Ooh, those are looking great," Reverie says to them, and the children beam at her with delight.

A few minutes later they reach one of the barricade sites. A tradesman of the town, a wildblood man with a feline nose and whiskers, offers a plan on how to arrange the materials in the most robust manner to create structures around eight feet high.

"Let's do it," Wren says with approval.

Hammers and nails are handed out, and Reverie holds hers at the edges of her fingertips while regarding it with something akin to distasteful fascination.

"Okay, and if I have *never* needed to use one of these before?" she asks.

"Hit the nail, and not yourself," Wren suggests. "And stick the wood with the pointy end." Reverie's eyebrow quirks in time with her mouth, and before she can speak again, Wren adds: "And no, we don't need another joke about how thick any of this wood is."

This draws laughter from the nearby carpenter and disdainful tutting from Lark.

Reverie only grins. "Noted." There is so much mischief in her eyes that Wren focuses on her own hammer before she fails to follow her own advice and crushes her own finger.

They work in what would be companionable silence if not for Reverie's humming. An hour later, the first section of the barricade stands strong.

"Pretty good," the carpenter says. "Next one!"

Lark sighs, perhaps without meaning to.

"Lark." Wren considers the way they are fidgeting, the shift of their feet and darting eyes and tapping of the hammer against their wrist. "Do you need to take a break? Walk around the block?"

"What?" Their eyes blink at her. "I—yes. A walk. Good. Good plan."

With that, they tuck their hammer and nails into a pocket in their coat, and stride off. Wren shakes her head fondly and gets back to work.

"They hate sitting still, huh?" Reverie asks.

"You could say that."

"You two make more and more sense all the time. Really effective duo. It's... neat."

For a wordsmith, it sure doesn't sound as though *neat* is the word that Reverie means. But for the life of her, Wren can't fathom which one she would be omitting.

Gods help Wren, though, she can't help but ask: "Neat?"

Reverie makes a face. "Well, I'm trying really hard to make friends with you, while trying to mind my own business. And I'm really awful at minding my own business."

Wren can only laugh at the honesty and the way Reverie's nose scrunches during the last sentence.

"Fair enough." Wren offers no more information, because if Reverie is avoiding questions about what Wren *thinks* she is, it is one of the last things Wren wishes to discuss.

"So, why haven't people been hailing you as a hero before today?" Reverie asks instead.

Which, you know. Is getting close to the *absolute* last thing Wren wants to discuss. With her heart kicking back into a gallop, Wren half bites her tongue and simply asks, "What?"

"Well, you're picture perfect hero material," Reverie says. "Muscles, gorgeous jawline, big sword. Heart of gold."

"Thanks," Wren says, considering that she has been debating how much she likes the changes she's made to her jawline through her affirmation elixir, and resolving to examine herself again in a mirror the first chance she gets.

"So, why is today the first day?"

Wren hammers a nail too hard. She takes the blow to her thumb without noise or wince. "What makes you so sure? That today is the first day?"

There is a pause and Wren glances up to see Reverie hesitant, her tongue wetting her lips. "Because it seemed like you didn't know how to handle it." No judgement. No accusation or pity. Just some sort of sympathy, simple and soft.

"I'll handle it fine," Wren says. "I just wasn't expecting it."

Reverie holds her gaze, as if not finished. The weight of words unspoken hangs heavy between them, but then she smiles as if nothing had happened at all.

"I bet you will."

Wren nods, awkwardly. "I'll go check that everyone's getting on okay with the other barricades. You can help these guys if they need anything, yeah?"

Reverie is quick to nod. "Sure. Whatever you need."

Wren smiles with gratitude, and exchanges nods with the carpenter and the others before she heads off. The next barricade is just enough of a walk that Wren can try to clear her head.

"No heroics, just saving a town," Wren mutters to herself. It sounds absurd even just under her breath, a contradiction in all but reality.

It is that obligation that she and Lark value so highly. There is little choice in any of it. Wren could never turn from this town, when she knows her time and sword could save lives within it. What may seem like heroics to some is merely the opposite of villainy to others.

Maybe trying not to be a villain is enough.

Wren is about halfway through the walk when she registers a scuffling noise from behind her, faint as anything. When she stops, it stops. When she resumes walking, it resumes.

Upon turning around, Wren sees none other than Ferdinand, the goose, staring back at her.

"No," Wren says, waving her hand at him. "Go back to Reverie."

He honks in a manner that gives the impression of *no, you can't make me*. And, unfortunately, he is completely right unless Wren wants to pick him up and throw him like a javelin.

Which, admittedly, is a tempting thought if what Reverie says about his telepathic commentary is true.

"Urgh," Wren says, and turns back to keep walking.

Watching the evil goose without his keeper had *not* been on Wren's list of expectations for the day, and it is the opposite of a nice surprise.

Chapter 7

By the time Wren and Ferdinand arrive at the next barricade, it's been started but needs another pair of hands. It's manned by several tired but eager teenagers who are busying themselves by throwing half-hearted crude jokes around with the nails.

Their jokes quiet down with Wren's arrival, but the longer she stays silent and pays them little attention, the more easily they slip back into their conversation and silliness. The last thing she wants to do is deny them any moments of happiness they can grasp.

It's a calming thing, to let the world come down to only the nail in front of her and the background chatter that merges into a sea of sound.

At least until there comes an awful shattering of wood. Then another. And another.

"What the—"

The teenagers and Wren search for the source of the sound, but see nothing. There is a thud of wood, something falling, and a groan of strain.

A section that had just been finished lurches and Wren hurries to hold it up before they lose all of their progress.

"Is that a goose?" one of the boys asks.

Oh by the Maiden's tits.

"Shit, hold this," Wren says to the teens, who hurry to do as she says while she curses herself for forgetting something crucial. She had to watch the goose.

Sure enough, when she moves around the barricade, she sees the smug bastard all but grinning at her before he grabs a nail in his beak and pulls it free.

Wren dives. The goose side steps. Wren eats plank.

To top it all off, her defeat is witnessed and is immediately met by a chorus of laughter from the teenagers holding the barricade together. Wren cannot even be angry, because with the last few days she knows they've had, any laughter they can grasp is to be treasured. She can let them have it, at her expense.

She cannot, however, let the feathered asshole continue honking in such a self-satisfied manner as he makes a break for it down the road out of town.

Thankfully, her legs are much longer than his, and catching him is child's play. She grabs him by the neck, more gently than he deserves, and holds him up so that they are eye to eye. He meets her gaze; beady eyes hold the brazen confidence of a creature with nothing to lose.

"No," is all she says, and this time the word is more of a threat than she has uttered to anyone in her life.

Ferdinand honks in her face.

"They might be back *today*, we need every minute we can get—"

Another honk. This one is back to sounding like laughter, and Wren feels her own foolishness smack her across the face, enhanced by a new horror. Reverie has tried to make it clear that this goose is truly an evil being, but such a thing is so difficult for Wren to comprehend. At least, until he laughs at the prospect of innocents being slaughtered due to his meddling.

Wren understands now that this is no matter of dramatic exaggeration. She is staring pure evil in the face, and it is a goose, and she has no idea how to beat him.

"Do I need to get Reverie to kill you again? So you stop endangering everyone here?"

The next honk sounds a lot like a *try it, bitch* if Wren had ever heard one. She is about to give up, and lament that if she cannot stop a goose, she has no hope of stopping Viken, when—

Something behind Ferdinand. Something perfect. Something that will at least make him hesitate before crossing her again.

Three steps and a crouch, and then the most hysterically funny sound from a goose she has ever heard, as Wren dunks him into a large and gloriously muddy puddle.

Once. Twice. Thrice. And then, she walks away, satisfied, as he tries to shake the mud off his feathers and honks after her with what she is sure are promises and wishes of painful death.

As Wren returns to the barricade, victorious for now, Norak is waiting with the teenagers, eyebrows nearly in his hairline as he gapes at Wren.

"Do I want to know what's going on here?" he asks.

"Probably not," Wren says. "But he was wrecking the barricade. I had to make a point. And he's not a regular goose. I'd never treat an innocent animal like that."

"It's true, Norak—I mean, sir—he was wrecking it real bad," one of the teenagers vouches. "No normal goose could do it so good, he knew all the bits to pull out."

"Shout if he tries anything else," Wren tells them, and the teenagers nod in eager unison.

It's jarring, being treated with any kind of authority, but that's hardly the biggest problem in this particular moment. Something to freak out about later.

"Is everything alright, Norak?" Wren asks, a bit more quietly, hoping the teens will get back to their work of barricade-building and goose-scouting. Which, helpfully, they do.

"The other barricades are doing well," Norak says, with a small smile. "It's good to see some hope around here again."

Wren nods, unsure of what to say.

"We've got meals getting cooked up in the inn," Norak says. "Pots of stew. The last of the bread. Please, come and help yourself soon."

"I will, don't worry," Wren assures him. "We just need to get these nails in to fix what the goose nearly wrecked."

He blinks. "Right. I'll help."

They do some quick work until the barricade is self-sufficient again, and then Wren is happy to leave the teens to it once they promise to swap out with her for dinner when she returns.

Wren looks at Norak as they walk, and finds him glancing at her in a similar way. The silence between them feels wrong, like they surely have things to say to one another.

They are so similar, more so than anyone Wren has encountered lately. But to remark on it would be admitting uncertainty, admitting fear at the dark about to close in on them.

"Are you okay?" Wren asks.

"Yeah," Norak says, but it sounds more instinctive than anything, and sure enough he pulls a face as soon as the word has left his mouth. "I mean, my town is under attack and everyone I've ever looked up to is too injured to help. And everyone is looking at me. So, you know, *no*."

"Good," Wren says. "If you were okay, I'd be more worried. Being not okay means you're a person in a shit situation."

Norak exhales, and for a single moment he lets his face crumple under the weight of his new responsibility, and Wren can only think *we are too young for this*. But then, is anyone ever old enough for such a thing?

The world is a wild place, where the duality of people is the only certainty, kindness and cruelty destined to always coexist. It is simply upsetting how many lives can be hurt by one cruel person gaining any power. It doesn't feel balanced at all.

Wren puts a hand on Norak' elbow and gives it a firm squeeze so that he can feel it in the gap between the metal plates of his armour.

"You're doing great," Wren says. "I bet your ma will be proud, when this is done."

Norak blinks watery eyes and nods, putting his hand back on his sword and letting his composure come back. "I—thanks."

Wren nods, and they walk the rest of the way in silence. By the time they reach the inn and join the lines for bowls of stew, Norak is back to being the picture of quiet leadership and strength.

The stew is simple and flavourful, and Wren considers the beauty of people huddled together, eating from the same pot that has been prepared with love and effort, with ingredients probably from the town's own fields.

"We still need a retrieval team," Norak says to Wren as they eat. "To get back the gold, whenever they attack."

"Right. People we don't want fighting, but who will be able to run if they get spotted," Wren says. "So... teenagers. Who don't have weapon skills, but want to help."

"What about the ones back at your barricade?"

Wren thinks it over. "They might be willing to give it a try. I'm not sure I know them well enough to say."

"Those three are tough, and good at getting out of trouble," Norak says. "I'll ask them."

They finish their food and head back to the barricade together. Wren hangs back while he asks the teens if they're interested in volunteering for the dangerous task, and they light up at the chance to do something so crucial instead of hiding with their families.

Wren half listens, half tries to shut it all out so that the guilt doesn't consume her. All she can do is hope with everything she has that they will return safe from this job that she created. If they do not, she knows she will not forget it or forgive herself easily.

The teenagers run off to grab some supplies and cloaks, and Norak coughs into his hand.

"I need to get everyone organised," Norak says to Wren. "You'll come to the square soon? To help?"

"Soon," she promises, and he gives her a tight smile before heading off.

With her newfound solitude, Wren examines the barricade and finds that the teenagers have done an excellent job of finishing it off, and is relieved to see the goose seems to have found something else to do because he is nowhere to be seen.

The first bit of movement on the horizon just looks like a trick of the dying light of day. But when Wren looks the second time, it is a person, moving at breakneck speed. Her hand goes to her sword on instinct, but there is no armour and no sign of blue on their person.

It's another young person from the town. Norak had mentioned that he would send some scouts out to ensure they don't get taken by surprise.

Wren climbs the barricade so that she can help him get up it, bringing him back onto the town side.

"They're coming," he pants immediately. "Gods, I got way too close. But it was worth it. An hour. They'll be here in an hour, and they're coming from the south side."

Chapter 8

Chaos breaks loose from there. News travels like a bad scent on the wind, and the able locals convene in the town square to be armed with every bow the town possesses. Others begin moving the injured, so they can hide in smaller, more spread out places.

Wren returns to the barricade where she had left Reverie, to see if she is still there, and finds her explaining something intricately arcane to Lark, who is doing a lot of nodding.

"Wren!" Lark calls. "I'm sure you've heard."

"I have an hour, and I know which way they're coming in," Reverie says, voice giddy with an excitement that Wren finds baffling, but encouraging. "This is a Disciplined mage's *dream*. I've got an incredible idea. I need to get to the southern barricade. I'll see you there!"

"Wait," Wren says, all at once flooded with alarm. "The goose. He was trying to wreck barricades, and I stopped him but I couldn't—"

"Oh, yeah," Reverie says, a furious shadow passing over her face. "Norak caught him trying to shit in the food supply. So he's gone now."

She does not elaborate, and Wren does not ask because truly what can one say to such a thing?

"Don't worry," Reverie says. "But I do need to go. Wish me luck!"

With that, she is gone in a whirlwind of colour. Lark and Wren stand, in a moment of calm before the storm.

"So, if I'm right, my uncle is here in an hour," Wren says.

Lark nods. Their face is impossible to read. "Yes. How does that sit with you?"

"I have to face him. And I might have to kill him."

"You don't have to face him alone. And you don't *have* to kill anyone you don't want to."

They make it sound so simple. But it is anything but, especially since it is *them* and she cannot forget the things she has watched them do, the things she has *helped* them do—

"I might be the only one who knows him *and* what he's done," Wren says. "So who else is going to do it?" She wonders if they hear the double meaning in the words, the reverse of it.

"There's always the justice system," Lark starts to say.

"Yes, and no one responsible for multiple murders of innocents has ever gotten out of that," Wren retorts before she can stop herself.

Lark blinks. "What is *that* supposed to mean?"

"It means I'm going to stop the murderer I'm responsible for," Wren says. "And I hope that the same goes for you, when we find yours." They open their mouth to speak and she holds up a hand to stop them. "What happened at the gate in Kequm was fucked. And I know I helped, but I did it for you. And I keep wondering if I should have."

"That is *not* the same."

"Isn't it? If we don't stop these people we still love, people who have hurt us, the blood of people we've never met will be on our hands. Seems the same to me."

"We do what we can, Wren," Lark says, voice pained. "Sometimes it isn't enough."

"No, sometimes it isn't *good* enough."

And then she does it again. Turns away so that they cannot speak, so that another excuse cannot leave their mouth, because it will do nothing to help. It is not kind of her to do, but Lark needs a reality check, a new perspective, or there will only be more disaster to come.

So she walks, and they follow in silence. There will be time later for them to try and resolve some of their mess, but the town is not guaranteed that same luxury.

Norak is running strategy in the square. Reminding them how to get good shots on the bows, advising them on which areas are easiest to hit on armoured targets.

"Wren," he says, looking relieved to see her. "Anything to add?"

Wren hesitates, alarmed at how many eyes turn to her. "Uh—yeah. I mean—" She curses herself, takes a deep breath, and tries again as she meets their gazes. "You do your best. You fire the shots. But if they make it over the barricade, you run. You keep that distance. They've trained for this for years, and you won't last if they get close. But they're not arrowproof, and Norak and I are going to do everything we can to hold them back for as long as we can. And we have two mages to match theirs, and one of ours is excited enough about what she's doing that I think they should be very, very afraid. The other one is going to keep you all fighting fit."

There is a ripple of curious excitement through the civilians, murmurs and hushes and brighter eyes as they grip their bows harder.

"We can do this," Wren says, if only to convince herself.

For the first time, she notices a secondary group who are waiting with nets, bricks, and a cache of other bizarre household items.

"What's happening over there?" Wren asks Norak.

"Oh!" Norak smiles at the group. "These guys said they can't shoot to save themselves, but they want to help. So they're going to set up on roofs near the barricade and just start throwing shit at anyone who makes it past."

"Oh," Wren says. "Yeah. Bricks can work, in a pinch."

"Ooh! I might have some other things!" Lark begins digging through their pockets, dumping things into Wren and Norak's hands. "That's a returning dart, here, sir, you give that a try—no, those seeds aren't any good they take at least two days to grow anything big enough—" They pull out a few glowing spheres the size of small apples, tilt their head, and shake it a moment later. "No, that's not going to help. Here, Norak, hold these, be careful, they explode—"

"They *what*?!"

"They explode if they hit something with enough force, big fiery explosion, so don't drop them, I'm nearly finished—"

"Why would you have something like that in your pockets?" Norak asks with bewilderment. "Isn't that dangerous?"

Lark blinks at Norak. "Well, they're insulated pockets. I do think things through, you know."

"Insulated with what?!" Wren can't help but ask.

"Aha! That's what I was looking for," Lark says as they pull out a small bead that Wren swears contains wisps of dark smoke. "Single-use darkness cloud. Great for a getaway." They hand it to a nearby interested woman who is part of the roof group. "Here. If things go poorly and people need to run, you can throw this from where you are. Should work, but hopefully you don't need it. Get it back to me if you can, I'll make use of it at some point."

They get a solemn nod in return, and Lark beams and begins grabbing back their pocket contents from Wren and Norak. In go the seeds, the spheres which Wren swears she hears Lark refer to fondly as 'boom balls', which surely cannot be their actual name, and about four other things that Wren is now too terrified to ask about.

Besides, Lark isn't the only one with magic to bring to the field.

"Just watch out for their mages," Wren says to the civilians, "in case they see you and start trying to hit you from further back. We know they probably have at least two, with the fire and the ice."

"I think the wooden barricades might have more to fear from, you know, the fire," one of them says.

Wren winces. "Well, it's all we've got."

No one looks reassured by this, and she cannot fault them for it. She can only look at the faces staring back at her and feel the weight of their lives hanging in the balance, threatening to fall onto her shoulders. She wishes she had more words, better words, anything. Something clever or funny that would ease their spirits for a moment, but it is not her way. Reverie is absent when she is direly needed for such a task.

Wren looks back at Lark, with every apology she can muster in her eyes, with a plea for help.

They cough to clear their throat, and when they speak, it is to everyone.

"All we've got? Ha!" Lark grins, so wide it might even be genuine. "All we've got is the information. The preparation. We know which way they're coming, and they don't know we know. We have me to make sure your acting captain and my friend Wren can hold that barricade against dozens of swords. If anyone does make it over, we have a mage who is setting up something that will make it hell for anyone to reach any of you. You have arrows. You have each other. And you have *everything* to fight for. If I were them, I'd be terrified. But they're not, because they think this is going to be easy. And I *love* it when they're wrong."

The atmosphere is intoxicating as they finish speaking, every person beginning to inflate with new hope and power, and the envy in Wren's chest as she looks at Lark nearly burns her alive.

"Let's give them the least polite Hanos welcome we've got!" Norak adds, and like a spark to kindling, the crowd erupts into cheers, whistles and applause.

The whole thing is so powerful that Wren wonders if she's the only one who gets an aftertaste of desperation from the noise as it fills the air. Only victory will get rid of it, so Wren swallows it down and feels her heartbeat kick up a notch.

It's happening. The bandits are really coming, and Wren will have to face Viken.

Wren looks to Lark, because she owes them that much after what they've just pulled off. "Let's go check on Reverie. Norak has it from here."

Lark nods. "Agreed."

"What's she doing, anyway?"

"Oh, you'll see. I just hope she gets it right."

Wren stares at them with horror. "You made it sound certain, back there!"

Lark sighs. "Well, it's what they needed to hear. She hasn't let us down yet—I'm putting my faith in her, but my hope also."

It makes enough sense, but everything is so messed up that Wren finds herself wondering if Lark has ever put such faith or hope in her, if she has done enough to make them believe in her so.

Would she even deserve it?

Her uncle's face swims in her mind, his strong cheekbones and beard, the ginger hair identical in colour to that of her father and brothers, the same green eyes. For a sickening moment, he's like a vision of what she could have been.

When her stomach turns, Wren isn't sure if it is rebelling against the idea of becoming a killer like him, or against her condemnation of him. Older, fonder memories pull at her: training with him and relishing in the extra difficulty of his challenges, drinking with him when she was old enough, sharing her new name with him and being hugged so fiercely she could scarcely breathe.

And then the cufflink. The tiniest thing, lying there in the mud as her vision blurred. The tiniest thing, that paired with all the other details, had shattered everything in a moment.

A hand touches her own, and Wren startles. She meets Lark's gaze.

"Wren," they say. "Your aura is—please. Talk to me."

"How do you bear it?" Wren asks, in a whisper. "Loving someone when you know they don't deserve it anymore?"

Lark swallows, hard. Their hand trembles where it is still touching her and quickly retracts. "I'll let you know when I figure it out. Rationality is hard to apply to the mortal heart, you know."

"You can *see* people's hearts," Wren says.

"I can see their emotions—and am extraordinarily bad at extrapolating implications from them," Lark corrects. "I shudder to think of the things that Miss Rosetia could glean from the world if she had the power of a green dragon."

Wren imagines it, and would indeed shudder if her chest weren't as heavy as a stone. "Why take the power, then?"

"Wren, this is me when I *can* see what people are feeling," Lark says. There is a hint of a wry smile on their lips. "Can you imagine how poorly I handled social situations before having that power?"

Wren laughs, a funny choked thing.

"I didn't seek it out," Lark continues. "But when the power to soften one of my larger weaknesses fell in my lap, I couldn't resist. And I'm glad I didn't. Being able to see when people are upset, or scared? See if they might need help? I wouldn't trade it easily."

Their hand twitches in her direction, the same one that had reached for her before.

"What can I do?" Lark asks plainly. "Anything I can do to make this easier for you, I'll do it."

Wren considers the offer for several moments, averting her eyes as she does so to avoid getting caught in the intensity of their gaze. "Keep the civilians alive, as many as you can. And do *not* get between me and my uncle."

She looks back so they can answer, and they surprise her by giving a wordless, solemn nod.

Wren wishes to touch them, to convey something she would struggle to put into words. But it is too intimate with the fears they have just voiced. She doesn't know how to do this, whatever this is—if it is anything at all. Sometimes Lark looks at her and there is *something* and Wren feels as though they are on some kind of tight rope, in danger of falling one way or another. But Wren has no experience, and Lark's heart is in the grasp of a petty, serial murderer.

If there is anything between them, and a time for it, that time is not now.

So all she says is, "Thank you."

Lark smiles at her, and Wren returns it. There is an entire moment where Wren believes everything will be alright.

But then, a group of civilians come past, children at their sides as often as not, bows on their back in favour of holding their children's hands a little longer. Reality crashes back in like an uncaring wave.

If this doesn't work, it will be all their fault.

Chapter 9

ONWARD TO REVERIE THEY go, following the civilians to the southern barricade. The barricade has been built in the space of what must have once been a gate, but now is nothing but hinges.

The colourful musician is walking a slow path around the large, circular symbol shining against the cobblestones. It's on the ground directly before the barricade, a ten foot radius intricate enough to make Wren dizzy just from looking at it.

Walking, however, is the wrong word for what Reverie is doing. She is stepping with the grace of a ballerina, feet turned out and fingers arched. The words she utters mean nothing to Wren and yet—somehow they feel like promises, of wonder and euphoria and spectacle that tug at something within Wren's gut. It's no more than that, perhaps because it's not finished.

It will never stop amazing Wren how utterly pink Reverie's magic is, how it can match the colour of her skin just as much as Lark's matches the gold of their scales. Lark had explained their theory on it once, something about magic being so innate in everything living that it attunes to a part of a person's essence. It makes enough sense for the draconic magic in Lark's blood, but something as simple as someone's skin or hair colour seems strange. But then, despite the demonic influence on her heritage, Wren knows that pinks and teals like Reverie's are indicative of elven blood, of old fey magic influencing the bloodline going back millennia.

Why does everything have to come back to magic? And how can Wren hold onto her exasperation when witnessing a sight like the one before her? The pale pink swirls around Reverie's body, tiny tendrils splitting off join the circle and its glow.

"It's fascinating getting to work closely with a Disciplined caster, again," Lark says to Wren when her eyes flick to them. "It's been a long time. I went to school with one. Remarkable woman. I'll have to go and see that adventuring guild she's helped set up, once all of this is done. Sounds fascinating."

They watch until Reverie steps away with a final flourish of her hand and a lingering note in her voice. For the first time, she glances in their direction and starts.

"Oh! Hey!" She glances between them and the circle with a kind of sheepish pride. "I think I did it right. I've only ever used my dad as a tester for it. Never had a chance to use it for real. But it got him pretty good."

"Is it harmful?" Lark asks.

Reverie grins. "Let's go with *debilitating*." It's not a good smile. It's a little too wicked, too excited, and Wren is alarmed to be reminded of Nightingale, the murderer. "The magic won't hurt them, but they'll be really easy to fill with arrows or knock out while it has them."

"Ah," Lark says. "That *is* helpful. And it won't affect the civilians?"

"Not if I can get the next bit right," Reverie says, and she reaches into her pack to grab her lyre. "Okay. Let's see."

She strums the lyre, a soft chord that matches the tone she had been singing as she drew the circle. She sings it a moment after, and the circle's magic pulses as if in response.

Some archers are preparing, standing in half-ready formations with their bows held loose at their sides. Others are sitting in family groups, using every moment they have to the fullest. Reverie steps around all of them, still singing, weaving her tune again, and despite their obvious confusion she does nothing but smile and keep going. After going around them, then she goes between them, weaving a trail of pink behind her with each step and note.

Norak arrives as this is going on, and is stuck watching Reverie for several moments.

"I—what is she doing?"

"No idea," Wren says. "But she says it's important for her spell."

Norak looks to Lark, who beams at the chance to speak.

"Oh, I have my theories, but I shan't take the stage from her when I might not even be correct," Lark says. "Her execution is marvellously uncommon."

"Norak," Wren says, as her attention is grabbed by something utterly different. "You have two shields. And an extra sword."

"Oh! Yeah, here," Norak says, offering the larger of the two wooden shields he's holding. "This is my mother's. She said to use it to protect the town."

Wren curses herself for not thinking about how obviously holding a barricade is going to work much better with a shield than her greatsword. As she kneels next to her bag, she fishes out her gauntlets and helmet.

Lark rushes to hold everything as she gets herself sorted, and in no time at all Wren is barricade-ready. Shield and a one-handed sword.

Norak pulls on his own helmet and nods in solidarity.

Reverie comes to weave through the three of them, singing all the while, stepping between them as though she has all the reason in the world to be doing so.

After circling them several times, she twirls on the spot and closes her melody with a soft descending scale.

"There," she whispers, after. "I think that will work."

"Couldn't the bandits just step around it?" Wren asks, not meaning to shatter the moment but unable to help herself. "If I were them, I'd try to go around it. It's obviously enemy-side magic."

Reverie makes a face. "Yeah, but I—" Her eyes spark. "Wren, can you help me test it? I have an idea, but I need to be sure."

"Sure," Wren says, feeling anything but.

Reverie grabs her hands and begins walking them both towards the circle, and it is everything Wren can do not to drag her heels.

"Me first, the caster," Reverie says as she steps backward over the border. There is a soft pulse, but nothing happens. "Then, someone I've aligned to the resonance. Which is *everyone here.*"

Wren meets her gaze, takes a deep breath, and steps into the circle. There is a tingle in her mind as the circle pulses again, and Wren can almost hear the melody Reverie had been singing, as if it were still playing.

Reverie beams. "*Yes.* Oh, thank the Inventor." She turns and looks to the children behind her, specifically the ones whose drawings she had complimented earlier in the day. "Hey, I need an awesome drawing right here, to cover up the shiny magic. Do you think you could do that? It might save the town."

The children—who look perhaps eight years old, four of them—stare at Reverie for a moment with wide eyes, before unstoppable grins take over their faces.

"We'll use the blue," one of them says, and runs forward before their nearby mother can stop them.

The other three dash away from their own parents, and all four stop short of the circle.

"So we can come in? You came in."

Reverie nods. "I was checking it was safe, for you. Do you guys have any spare? I might help, if that's okay."

"Sure!"

The five of them get to work with the chalk, creating an intricate and nonsensical chalk design on top of the magical runes.

"I'm still not sure I understand how this can ignore us but hurt the bandits," Wren says. "What do you mean by the resonance?"

"That's how my ma explains it," Reverie says. "Magic is in everyone, everything, right? I can use the resonance to sort of... put us all in the same key. I made the spell with one song, and then expanded it and wove it through everyone here. So now, everyone here is tuned to the same resonance, so we don't trigger the spell. But those bandits will."

She grins at Wren and Lark both, and wordlessly allows one of the children to swap chalk colours with her.

"Fascinating, I usually focus on individual essences. I can't set things up to trigger later," Lark says.

"Gifted versus Disciplined." Reverie seems delighted. "Wild."

"Well, it sounds great," Wren says. "Can't wait to see it."

Reverie beams. "Me too." She looks around, taking everything in with a more somber expression. "So, it's happening, then? Bandits? Fighting? Elemental mages?"

"Yeah," Wren says, wishing she could think of the right thing to say for once in her life. "Your spell should make a big difference."

"I hope so." Reverie glances at the circle and its chalk adornments, and smiles at one of the beaming children still working on it. "Never gotten a chance to help so many people before. Not like this."

Lark nods, their eyes following a path around the circle before finding Reverie's face again. Their lips twitch. "Consider this your heroic debut."

Reverie laughs while Wren has to hold in a wince. The very word 'hero' seems determined to attack every part of her chest, every inch of anxiety and inadequacy.

"A Seeker and a Rosetia, backing up a—" Reverie stops short and gives Wren a smile that has no right to be so adorable. "A Wren. With a giant sword. Awesome."

Wren could kiss her for not saying the word. Or cry. She does neither, though, and instead squares her shoulders and nods as if there is little to worry about.

"I'll tell you what I told Lark," Wren says. "Don't get between me and my uncle."

Reverie blinks. "Oh. Sure."

"Thank you."

As the three of them look around at each other, something calms in Wren's chest. Where before she stood utterly alone, now any solitude will be by choice.

"That's the signal!"

The shout comes from the barricade, and sure enough, the speck of bright magic on the horizon is the agreed signal of the bandit approach. The townsfolk leap to action, with the children hurrying to follow their school teacher back into the depths of the town, to their agreed hiding places. There are fleeting final goodbyes and see-you-soons, and the archers begin to prepare their opening shots.

Wren climbs the barricade alongside Norak and stands at its peak, looking out at the force of several dozen coming into sight even as dusk seeps through the sky.

"Here we go," Wren says, under her breath. Then, louder, and to the archers, "Hold your arrows until they're close!"

Reverie has grabbed a bow and joined the archer's ranks, and seems to at least be holding it right. The others have reached their positions on the outmost roofs.

Lark climbs the barricade up to the second highest step, and touches Wren and then Norak in turn, on the shoulder both. Their other hand holds their holy symbol of the Scholar. Against the sound of footsteps coming closer, their prayer is the only other thing filling the air.

"Scholar, these are protectors of the innocent, protectors of history and independence and geography. This place is its people, their knowledge only safe in *their* safety. Scholar, preserve them. Battle Maiden, guide us. Let these bastions hold the line."

The magic is warm, as always, and Wren sees Norak fidget with surprise as it takes hold.

"Weird," he murmurs. "But I'm guessing... helpful."

"You wondered how I beat ten of them," Wren says. "That's how." She looks at Lark, and the beads of sweat that have broken out on their forehead. "Won't this exhaust you?"

Lark shrugs. "The longer you two hold, the better our chances. It's worth the strain. I'll be alright."

"Hold," Norak calls to the archers, as the bandits draw near and Lark drops back to the town side's ground level. "Almost. Almost... *release!*"

The arrows fly, and the bandits screech as they are rained on by sharp metal. Only a couple of unlucky ones drop from the first shower, but many are slowed in their advance—if only to yank the shafts out of shallow, unimportant wounds.

In their position on a makeshift flat platform in the barricade's centre, Wren and Norak are as much of a wall as the rest of the barricade itself. It comes with significant risk of making themselves targets for the enemy mages, but that will force the mages to reveal their identities and locations.

It's tricky, a skirmish like this. Wren is resolved to never kill another where it can be helped, and she is well-practiced in hitting places that are effective for disabling and not fatality. But battle is a fast thing. Wren has to prioritise her side's survival before all else. And, ultimately, lives lost in battle such as this, between equal opponents, is an utterly different thing to murder in other circumstances.

The bandits reach the barricade. The world turns to a noisy din.

Fighting with Norak, side by side, feels better than anything she can remember. Not another mage, but another person armed with only steel and skill and the will to stand up for those who cannot. The tandem slashes of her sword alongside Norak's blade feel so right that she loses herself to the rhythm. Slash, block, dodge, slash. Repeat.

There is only one problem, as they hold their ground perfectly. No magic comes their way. Not one blast of fire, not one cascade of ice.

"There's no mages here," Wren says to Norak. "We should have been hit by now."

"Shit." Norak blocks an incoming hit and becomes locked with the blade of a bandit on the steps below. "You're right, they must be somewhere else—"

"I'll find them," Wren tells him. "You stay with your people. Hold as long as you can."

Norak nods. He grimaces with determination and roars in the face of his attacker, forcing their blade back and making them lose their footing and fall off their meager foothold. "We will *not* yield!"

His shout is met with cheers from the archers. Wren waits for breathing room and leaps off the barricade, back towards the archers. Once again, Reverie's chalk covered spell does nothing to her when she lands in it. The mage herself is holding her own with the archers, a fascinating contrast in the textbook way she holds it, theoretically better than the townsfolk, but a lack of experience making each shot and reload too stilted, too slow.

Lark is nearby and moves to intercept Wren immediately as she begins to move through the group.

"Wren," they say, in between the words of their repeated prayer. Their hair is beginning to stick to their head with sweat.

"There's no mages," Wren says. "I'm going to find them. Drop the magic off me and keep it on Norak, he's going to need it."

"You'll be on your own," Lark says with an adamant shake of their head, and murmurs a few more lines of prayer before adding, "I'll keep it on you as long as I can."

"But you prioritise him," Wren says. "The barricade has to stand."

Lark's loathing of the situation shines through their eyes, a battle of wills that makes a storm. It rages with ferocity Wren could not have prepared for.

"Go," Lark says, quickly. "Before I change my mind."

Wren nods once and runs in the opposite direction. Lark's prayer behind her becomes almost aggressive, almost a demand of the Scholar and his sister the Battle Maiden. Hopefully that won't earn them any ill graces with the knowledge gods.

Wren's heart pounds in her chest as she dashes through the streets alone. She is not sure it has anything to do with the exertion of running through armour, but she throws the helmet off regardless, needing to feel air on her face.

Finding the mages should be simple. Elemental mages are not subtle by nature; Wren waits for flashes of fire, crackling of ice, columns of smoke. There is nothing. It makes so little sense that she wants to scream.

"Where are you?" she asks, under her breath. "What are you doing? Where—"

A group charge into the street ahead of her. Armoured, and with blue sashes. And at their head, grinning the moment she sees Wren, Darla.

Wren's heart drops into her stomach.

The mages cannot be far, because someone had to have freed them all from the guard house, but that will have to wait.

"Perfect," Darla says, and she begins to advance with the others keeping to her flank.

At least until there is a crash behind her and an explosion of flame covers the bandits, screams filling the street and sending them scattering to the wind until Darla is the only one that remains.

Wren and Darla, in simultaneous bewilderment, search for the source of the fire and see a middle-aged muscular orcish woman with a bandaged torso leaning against a house down the street, looking immensely pleased with herself. Her grin is so identical to that of Norak that Wren has no illusions of who this reckless warrior might be.

Wren can only grin back, especially when Darla's head whips back around to scowl.

"Gods help me, I'm going to make sure there isn't enough left of you for them to ever know," Darla mutters, and it's more chilling to realise that it's a promise to herself rather than a threat to Wren.

And yet, there is a simple fact that stops that chill from setting in, that prevents fear from seizing Wren where it has the last two times she has faced Darla.

"You know, you're in my way," Wren says. "And you've made it clear you place no value on mercy. You only left me alive to save your own skin."

"You're no good at threats, girl."

An odd part of Wren wants to giggle with inappropriate delight. She often thinks she had so little time to be a girl, that she went straight to being a woman, that where Darla means it as an insult it only sparks joy.

"No, I'm not," Wren says, voice quiet as she smiles. "Just good at pointing out the obvious that others miss."

And then, she charges Darla with no ceremony, no announcement, and almost catches her off guard for it.

The sword and shield are still in her hands, not her first arms of choice, but at least Darla and her shortsword have no experience of her fighting with them. It creates a different rhythm to their previous clash.

Darla's speed is her danger, as it has always been, but she needs precision to be able to hit Wren between her armour plates. With the shield to protect further, it's an extra challenge.

One thud against the shield. Another. A good feint, which Wren absolutely falls for, and Darla catches Wren's sword arm with a quick swing back. It lands on the metal plates, but the force of it hurts like a bitch even through Lark's protection.

Wren pushes forward with the shield, to test her balance, and brings her sword around to try and catch Darla while her balance is off. It almost works, but Darla is so quick, able to twist in a fraction of a moment to avoid the worst of the strike.

Block. Blow. Dodge. Strike. They trade tiny victories. It's not enough. Not for Wren, not for Darla. Something has to change.

Livid and just a little desperate, Darla's strikes are too wild. But all she needs is one good hit, and Wren might be in trouble depending on how long Lark's magic holds.

Besides that, Wren simply does not have the time to be stuck with Darla when the mages and her uncles are potentially still on the loose.

One idea. Absurd, and perhaps just unexpected enough that it may work.

Wren plants her feet in the ground and shoves Darla with the shield, forcing her to stumble backward and land in the dirt. Wren drops the one-handed sword to the ground and uses her free hand to grab the shield like a discus and throw it directly at Darla's head.

Darla's free arm comes up to protect her face, and the thud is still resonant as she groans and drops back into the dirt. Her other hand still grips her sword, and it comes up in wild swings, but Wren kicks it away.

"You leave me no choice," Wren says, feeling ill just at the thought of what must come next.

Darla's arm drops to show eyes filled with horror as Wren squares her jaw and brings her boot down on Darla's sword hand with force that makes the bone crack.

The yell from Darla echoes through the street. Wren is sure she won't forget it for a long time, the sound of such visceral pain caused by the brutality of her own strength.

"Hopefully this doesn't cause permanent damage," Wren says as she grabs the shield again. "But like I said. Mercy."

She brings the shield down on Darla's head, too direct for her arm to do any good, and knocks the other woman out cold.

Wren's gaze goes back to the still, mangled hand she broke. There's fighting, and then there is... violence like that. But leaving Darla able to hurt anyone else had not been an option.

She sighs and looks back to Norak's mother, skin crawling at the idea of having an audience to the whole ordeal. The other woman is watching and simply gives a nod.

"Did you see who let them out?" Wren asks.

"He went that way." She jerks her head, and begins limping closer. "Hope you weren't going to leave my stuff in the middle of the street."

"I—"

The older woman snorts. "Go. I've got it. And yes, then I'm going back to the hall. I think I pulled my stitches." A dark patch spreading across her bandages tells Wren that it's likely indeed.

"Be careful," Wren says.

"You're the one going after that tough bastard. Seems like he's the one in charge."

"Yeah, he is." Wren draws her own sword from her back, relieved to feel the weight of it back in her hands after wielding other arms. "Wish me luck."

"Everything the gods can give you."

They part ways. Wren heads down the street she had indicated, and has barely been walking for two minutes when a figure steps into the street from one of the alleys. Full plate armour. Blue sash. Helmet that hides anything distinctive from a distance. A tall, wide stature. Wren would know it anywhere.

"Uncle," she whispers.

He is a good fifty feet away, and doesn't seem to have noticed her. It's strange; coming in to free his people makes enough sense, but with that done, why is he skulking the backstreets? The way his helmet is rotating suggests he's examining the buildings as he walks, but why?

He strides off to the northwest, and Wren waits a sensible ten seconds before following at a slow pace with her hand pressed to the noisiest joint of her armour to minimise its clanking.

Whatever she had imagined his destination to be, the town's small library had not been it. He walks in as if it is the most natural place in the world for a fully armoured bandit leader to be.

Wren slips in a minute later. His rummaging in the office near the entrance is immediately audible.

The time is now. He's here, so is she, and they're both armed. He cannot deny any of it, caught in the midst of it all. So, naturally, she feels as though she is going to vomit. Can she actually step in and face him, condemn him, and hope to walk out alive or emotionally sound, let alone both?

It's delusion. But it is the right thing to do. Wren braces herself to see that face, to be bombarded by memories, and steps inside the room despite it all.

The helmet is on the desk. The figure turns as she enters. His mouth forms the shape of her old name, but it is not uttered, it is simply an old memory quickly discarded and replaced by—

"Wren?"

Wren cannot fault him for the near slip. The name on her lips had also been the wrong one. It's her uncle, but not the one she had been expecting.

Chapter 10

ALL THIS TIME, WREN has been preparing to see Viken, her father's brother. The owner of the cufflink, the one who had inspired her father to forge the sword he would later pass down to her.

Instead, she sees the man who is not her uncle by blood, but by marriage.

"Vasil," Wren says, numbly. Her own foolishness jeers at her, cruel in its victory over her. She had said herself that they wear matching armour, that their statures are near identical.

It's only now, this close and with the helmet off, that Wren can see the dark skin and eyes of Vasil, and not the features so close to her own. It hurts almost as much, him being in her life just as long as Viken. The only comfort is the absolute bewilderment written across his face; her own surprise is a molehill compared to his.

"Where's Viken?" Wren asks before he can recover.

"Gone," Vasil says, still stunned. He shakes his head. "I mean—gone ahead. He left me to finish things up here."

Wren has known this man her whole life, laughed with him and her family, always considered him one of them. Shared drinks with him, laughed at her brothers and their romantic missteps with him, poked fun at his husband together. The way he talks about his part in what is happening as if it is as mundane as a business transaction? It's maddening.

"When you say finish things up here," Wren says, allowing her face to betray her fury. "You mean, take the last bits this place has to give you? Like at home?"

Vasil, finally, has the grace to look abashed. "... yes. I suppose that is what I mean. But this place is special, Wren. There's something nearby worth more than this whole town. Help me find it. We could take it to Viken together, he'd be so delighted to see you—"

Wren can only ignore the outlandish nature of that suggestion. Instead, she asks, "What is it that you're looking for?"

"We've been, apparently, paid outrageously to retrieve something from the centre of a labyrinth," Vasil says, lighting up with excitement. "An ancient construction in local legend, supposedly built to protect a power source capable of things we can scarcely imagine."

"Week I've had, I can imagine quite a lot," Wren interrupts. "You want me to help you find it?"

"I'm not the only one looking. There's blood all over the desk as if someone was here first and killed the librarian, which could mean the information is gone—but I'm confident we can find the scraps we need."

There is odd vindication in knowing that she knows what he doesn't, that a woman beyond perhaps even his reckoning has beaten him to it. But she isn't one to brag, not when she could tell him nothing at all.

Besides, there is one awful word in his utterings that catches her by the gut.

"We," Wren whispers. "You *really* think I would help you with *anything* after what you two and your people did? I *knew* it was you, they all said I was deluded and seeing things but I *knew*. But you didn't even deny it just now."

"It wasn't personal, Wren," Vasil says.

"It was personal to *me*!" Wren never raises her voice, but there is an edge to it now that is deadly sharp. "Your people left me beaten. Bruised. Bleeding. Just for trying to defend my home."

Vasil's jaw squares. "Yes. Because they'd been told that if they harmed our family, Viken would take a hand, if not their heads. But we also have our policy about dealing with those who bear arms against us. They found a middle ground that we didn't care for, but found... adequate."

"Adequate," Wren repeats. "Was that his word? Or yours?"

"Does it matter?" If Wren didn't know better, she'd have said his voice is tinged with regret.

Perhaps it doesn't. Her humiliating defeat, injuries that had taken weeks to heal... adequate, in their eyes, likely both even if only one had used the word.

"Why?" Wren asks. "Why do it? Any of it? You were good mercenaries, why turn to hurting innocent people?"

"We're not trying to hurt anyone, Wren," Vasil says. "The casualties are minimised if we scare them enough to not fight back, trust me."

"Not for a second."

"We just want the gold, the valuables." Vasil sighs, his fingers trailing over the smooth wood of the desk. "But people don't tend to just hand them over. The rule of nature is that the strong take what they will, this is no different."

Wren stares at him. "Why do you need *so much*?"

Vasil blinks, opens his mouth, and says nothing. His dark eyes shine with something she cannot identify. Shame? Empathy? Something else altogether, perhaps.

"Because we can take it, now," he eventually says. It sounds weak. Like an echo of someone else's words. Viken.

"Now?"

Vasil, holding her gaze, murmurs a mere word and forms a flurry of ice around his hand as his eyes flash pure white. "Yes. Now."

Wren blinks. "*You're* the ice mage? But you were never a mage—"

"Until one day, I was. And the same day, Viken's magic manifested as well. Fire, brighter than his hair in its youth. Fire and ice." There is a soft, sentimental curl to his lips as he regards the magic around his hand. "We have always been perfect opposites, and our magic agreed."

Wren doesn't know enough about magic to say that it sounds like horseshit. She wishes she could, because instead she aches to think of how she had always thought of them as such, the perfect opposites, the perfect couple. It cuts deep into her chest, to see the model couple of her family become this. To see the sentiment unchanged but with a horrifying new backdrop.

"Leave," Wren says. "You were a part of my family just like Viken, so I'll offer that once. Leave, and take your people. The next time I see you, you won't get that offer."

Vasil blinks at her, even as she raises her sword. "Don't be ridiculous, Wren. If you aren't joining me, you'd best not be barring that door by the time I've found what I want."

Neither threat taken seriously. Both trying to brush off the other. Both headed for disaster.

Wren takes a deep breath and raises her sword up and back past her shoulders, ready to swing forward. "Leave. You aren't getting a single thing else out of this town."

"I don't want to hurt you, Wren," Vasil warns.

"But you will," Wren says, having to refrain from spitting at his feet. "Because that's just who you are, now."

His face twists. The flurry of ice in his hand bursts in a flash of white and cold, forcing her back a step just in time to dodge the swing of his handaxe.

"And who are you, now?" Vasil demands, his face coming through the faint mist of ice. "So far from home? Helping random, pathetic people for... what?"

"Does calling them pathetic make it easier?" Wren asks, which only makes the fury in his eyes burn hotter. Their weapons meet. Her sword is almost laughably huge compared to his axe.

Wait. His axe. She remembers something important a second too late—

He's always been a two-weapon fighter. One axe should have been suspicious, without the second on his belt, but it all makes sense now as she sees the spike of ice that has grown over his other hand. The ice is headed straight for her exposed side, the gap underneath her breastplate.

Too late for Wren to move. It finds a home and Wren cannot stop the groan she lets out. It's not as bad as it could have been, with Lark's magic holding it at bay just enough, but that is a small mercy.

Besides, the magic covering her is starting to feel weaker. Less warm. Almost flickering. Wren can almost picture how Lark might be knelt in the dirt, sweaty and bloody from the exertion of pushing themself too far.

But she cannot think of Lark now, not when she has to push Vasil back to get free of the ice shard.

All at once, Wren wishes she had sparred with him more in the past. It had always been Viken, with him being everything she wished to be, other than a man. Who better to learn from, than someone who wields the weapon that had inspired hers?

But a real fight is more than offense, or even the defense of your own weapon. It is the weapons of the others, the techniques that come with them, and how they make those techniques their own. Mages who were warriors first are much rarer than a skilled warrior, and ones that have learned to integrate their dual skillsets are rarer again.

Wren has never fought anyone like Vasil. Just when she thinks she has a good swing, her sword meets ice that forms around his arm like a shield. He then has the axe ready to swing around and catch her, and Wren barely avoids getting a matching wound on her other side.

His weapons catch hers and force her backward against the librarian's desk. Her bones rattle against her armour and the hardwood.

Wren braces herself and drives her head up into his, a vicious headbutt that sends them both reeling. The moment of stagger is all she needs from him to bring her knee up between his legs with as much force as possible. He hisses through his teeth at the low blow. Wren feels no guilt over dirty tactics when he has proven himself to have no honour.

Onto her feet with a push off the desk, she turns herself so her shoulder pauldron meets him first and forces him back.

The reality is that fighting in a small office is simply not what greatswords are designed for, and that if she had been expecting to face off against an ice mage of this ferocity she would have kept the damn shield. But Wren is adaptable, if nothing else. Her legs and shoulders serve her just as well.

Vasil is still unsteady, so she raises her blade and charges him.

He might have gotten her last time, but now she is the one on the offensive. She has no doubt her strength matches his.

His axe and ice shard meet her blade but they only slow her. She is an unstoppable force—so by the logic of something Lark had explained once, Vasil must move.

Sure enough, his balance wavers, and something deep within Wren sings with triumph as he is forced to step back. Once. Twice. Three times and his back hits the bookshelf.

With each strike, she waits for his face to twist and betray his contempt, the ugliness that has brought him so far. Surely, it can only lie so deep. But it doesn't come. He is frustrated, about to hit back, determined not to back down. But there is nothing else.

"Where's Viken?" Wren demands. "If this power source is so important, why leave?"

"I don't need his help." Vasil breaks his weapons free of her lock. "He had other matters to attend to."

His axe comes around, his ice shard right behind, but Wren has worked out his rhythm. She blocks, one and then the other, quick enough that he is completely exposed.

And then comes a moment, catching her off guard, where things are very simple. If she brings her blade down now, he dies, and she wins. The bandits will be without a leader. This town's nightmare is over.

Simple.

Except that he's her uncle, he's a person, and it's never simple. Wren falters, not moving her sword an inch, and a shiver runs down her spine. At first she thinks it's her own nerves, protesting the situation, but the lack of warmth lingers.

Lark's magic. It's gone.

As Wren exhales a breath of worry, Vasil breathes in the same air. It's a deep inhale, strangely so, but she thinks nothing of it until it comes back out in ice so dense and freezing it might as well come from a dragon.

Wren's face screams with the pain and shock of it. She can't see, can't think. And worst of all, the moment after it hits, the icy shard makes contact with her body again, sliding between the armour plates and sinking into her skin.

Wren is not sure she'll ever feel warm again. The world spins and she wonders if she has lost it all.

Chapter 11

It's been a little too long since Wren took a proper hit. A true blade, between her armour, with no magic to soften it. Everything about this instance is as bad as it could be; an attacker she loves despite herself, an attacker she could have killed before they got this far, her body screaming from the cold he has exhaled all over her.

If she had just been decisive, if she had not hesitated in the moment she needed to act—

Like right now. She needs to act right now.

Wren drops and rolls, her hand scrambling along the ground for anything on the floor to throw back in his direction. Her fingers rush over books too bulky to get a hold on, before finding something smaller. Solid, triangular... a paperweight?

She throws it behind her, blindly but with every bit of force she can muster, before rolling back to her feet and trying to blink the ice from her eyes. It stings like a bitch, but the room comes back to her in shapes and shades.

Foolish, Wren tells herself. *So fucking foolish.*

But there's another voice in her head too, persistent and cheerful. Norak. *I think everyone knows what their way is. Deep down. It's in your gut, your heart. You know what's you and what isn't.*

Wren considers Vasil, who is now clutching his head, as if the paperweight might have found better purchase than she had expected. She considers the wound in her side, making the world blur at the edges.

She cannot, for everything in her, find regret at not ending his life. Only for expecting herself to be able to, when it is not her way. She needed a different plan, a plan of her own, and came in without one.

Wren seeks revenge because that is what every story and heroic person she has met has told her she ought to do. But why must revenge be death? Why must she compromise herself for their faults?

Vasil is still where she had left him, sweat shining along his face alongside the blood beginning to drip.

Damn, Wren thinks, *what a shot.*

"I don't know a lot about magic," Wren says. "But I know you can only use so much before you have to rest. There's ice all through this place, from the last attack, and you haven't been gone a full day. So how much magic do you have left?"

Vasil answers her question with a charge right at her, and the air near her erupts into ice shards in the same instant.

Wren takes the only viable path, but at great risk. She rushes forward, away from the ice and towards Vasil, but ducks at the exact moment to send him perfectly rolling over her back with the right pull.

Her sword comes around in a powerful swing. It winds up right on course for where his neck meets his shoulders, and she prepares to stop it at the last moment, to put the fear of the gods into him—

The blade meets a wall of ice that shatters on impact. The greatsword point lands on his clavicle with a fraction of its original force, nicking his skin where it might have severed head from body.

The air is still. There is only their breath, and the ice falling around them, and the disbelief in Vasil's eyes. Wren doesn't need to kill him to win, only to have the opportunity. Vasil doesn't need to know that she won't seize it. All he knows is that Wren is the victor today.

How easy it could have been, to have killed him by accident, or for her hand to have been forced by self-defense. Instead, his life is in her hands again, his breath fogging her blade, his eyes stubborn as they hold hers.

"Well?" he asks. "Is it justice, for me, then?"

This is not the final option that taking a life ought to be, in her eyes. This is not her time to force the hand of justice, not her right to judge another mortal for their very mortality. And yet, he and Viken are her responsibility, and will hurt others if she does not stop them.

These can all be true, and all drive her to near madness, and it may be a while yet before she can reconcile them.

She breathes now because they told their people not to hurt their family. And that's the thing. She can't take a life where they ensured that she was spared.

"Here's what will happen." Wren speaks slow. Precise. She never breaks his gaze. "You'll leave. You'll go to your people, sound the retreat, and go to Viken. And you'll tell him that you failed because I beat you."

Vasil licks his lips. "Is that it?"

"It is," Wren says. "But the next time I see you and Viken, I'm putting an end to all of this."

Vasil laughs, arrogance burning in his eyes. "You catch me on my only day I'm overstretched, and won't make the most of your victory. You can't take me at my best, let alone Viken, to say nothing of *both* of us. Especially if you lack the strength to finish us off."

Naturally, he assumes that she plans to fight them head on and win, that she plans to kill them another day. The way the stories say she should. The way she won't.

Wren presses her sword more firmly against his neck, drawing more blood. "Your rules saved me. So now I'm sparing you, because we're family. But that can only go so far."

Vasil's eyes flash with something. "Very well. May I go?"

There is a beat. "Try anything, and you never reach Viken," Wren warns. "I'm not here alone. You should check on your people. My friend was confident her Disciplined magic would do a number on them, and my Gifted friend will be keeping everyone nice and healthy."

That seems to surprise him. He glances in the direction of the southern barricade, jaw much more tense than a moment ago. When he looks back, he nods once.

Wren retracts her sword from his neck and steps back. She waits for him to move.

Vasil sheathes his weapons first; the ice around his hand melts and creates a puddle on the stone floor. He takes a breath and heads for the door, but stops with one foot through it.

"Are you sure about that message?" he asks.

"I'm sure," Wren says. "Go. Now."

He sighs, and walks out. Wren waits until she is certain he is not coming back, and then lets herself fall against the bookshelf. She is battered, impaled, and drained. But she won.

In this moment alone, Wren allows herself a few tears for the mess of it all. For having to fight Vasil at all, for having him hurt her as badly as he has, for the prospect of fighting he and Viken in the future and probably losing. She can hope there is another way, but there is no guarantee.

Her uncle Viken, now a fire mage? Burning towns to take their wealth out of some entitlement, but trying to avoid excessive casualties? Would the world ever make sense again?

Her injury is winning now. Her hand touches it, between the armour plates, and comes away crimson.

Wren stares at it with morbid fascination as she slides down the bookshelf to the floor. The last time she had been stabbed—which had only been yesterday, and by a cranky old lady—she had not been lucid enough to consider the injury.

With Lark's protection gone from her, and the pain at the time, it certainly feels as though the injury should have been worse. Unless... Vasil hadn't been aiming for a fatal hit. Just a winning one. It's a dangerous thought, one laced with hope and uncertainty. She cannot linger on it, or on the way he had never quite given into the horrible parts of him she had expected to see. It would have been so much easier if he had been less than how she remembered him.

Wren has seen the damage done by love that refuses to let go. By a history of connection, by care for someone getting in the way of action, even in the face of the most awful deeds. She must be strong for herself, and for Lark. The group cannot handle more than one person being in that turmoil. She must be the common sense. Lark and Reverie certainly won't be.

She knows she needs to move, to find Lark and get healing, but her body feels so heavy. A small rest, surely, would be better so that it doesn't aggravate her wounds. Surely.

There is the smallest of quiets, then. It is broken slowly, like a dawn, by the sound of her name. Again, again, again.

Her eyes open to meet mismatched ones she knows well, the brown one bloodshot from exertion while the draconic green shines as bright as ever.

"Wren," Lark says, their voice not the one that had been speaking a moment ago. Their face takes up her whole vision, creased with worry while their smooth hands cup her face between them.

Wren's heart pounds in her chest. Guilt, for the worry caused. Shame, for the complicated emotions of it all. And, you know, that other thing that would have flushed her face if she weren't dealing with blood loss elsewhere.

"Hey," she says, with a smile. "Good timing. I got stabbed."

"Yes, I can see that from *the blood all over you*," Lark says with such fervent exasperation and hand flapping that Wren chokes out a laugh. "I told you this would happen!"

Wren takes a moment to look away from them, to seek out Reverie, who must have been the one initially saying her name, and finds her quietly examining the ice covered bookshelves. She gives Wren a small wave when their eyes meet.

"Did Norak hold the barricade?" Wren asks, looking back to Lark.

"I—well, yes, of course he did—"

"Then it was worth it."

Lark grumbles and goes about finding the most passive aggressive wording to a healing prayer that she's yet to hear, something about 'please heal this person who prizes the assets and lives of others above her own, who lost your protection when she needed it most'.

"So it seems like there was some kind of retreat," Reverie says. "You know anything about that?"

"Sounds lucky," Wren says.

"Mm." Lark lifts an eyebrow. "Your uncle?"

"My other uncle. His partner. I was so busy thinking I'd see Viken, I never thought it would be Vasil. But they're the mages. Both of them."

An odd laugh bubbles in Lark's throat. "That *would* explain the ice crystals on your armour."

For the first time, Wren can see how drained Lark looks, their skin washed out and blood staining the edges of their nostrils. They sway where they are crouched in front of her, and she grabs their shoulders to hold them steady.

"So you got stabbed and he left," Reverie says, some way off as she asks the question, circling the desk with a curious eye. "Who won?"

"I did," Wren says. "Just. And I don't think I will, next time. Got lucky."

"Then next time, you'll have us." Reverie glances at the blood covered desk. "Huh. I know Norak said the librarian died, but that's... a lot of blood. Sounds silly to say."

"I don't have proof, but I'm sure it was Nightingale," Wren says. "Vasil says the librarian might have had information about a labyrinth. Something nearby that guards a huge magical power source."

Lark nods rapidly. "I'd need to see the body to be sure. But everything fits. A day ahead of us, with an objective we know nothing of, and she kills the person most likely to know more about a hidden labyrinth than anyone else. We'll have to follow her, of course."

"Do we have any idea of where to go?" Reverie asks.

Wren shrugs, and is ordered to stay sitting and rest. Lark and Reverie meanwhile enter a flurry of investigation and overturning.

It's a relief to get ten minutes of respite, where Wren can close her eyes and let the sounds around her lull her into almost sleep.

A tap on the shoulder rouses her.

"There's only the smallest of references," Lark says, with a huff. "They all seem to agree the labyrinth lies in the hills directly east, and underground. But none of the local texts say *where* any possible entrance might be. And Rosetia, what in the world are you doing with that drawer?"

Reverie, whose hands indeed have been buried deep in the top drawer of the librarian's desk for the last five minutes, grins at them both.

"Well, if I was the local expert on something so dangerous," she says, "I wouldn't leave the important secrets where any greedy bitch could find it. I'd have an awesome, secret compartment in my desk."

"Yes, but *you* have a deeply uncommon flair for the dramatic that most lack," Lark says, snorting.

"That was *so* close to a compliment—"

"Fascinating that you interpret it that way, but unless you've actually found something—"

"There's an inch unaccounted for," Reverie interrupts, raising her voice to win the exchange. "Between the bottom of the drawer on the inside, and the bottom on the outside."

"And it couldn't possibly just be the thickness of the wood?"

Reverie's grin gets mischievous. "I *always* account for the thickness of wood. That's why I'm so popular."

She winks at Wren, who nearly chokes on her laugh. Lark rolls their eyes and shoves their hands in their pockets with exasperation.

"Well when you find something tangible sometime this year, let me know—"

There is a small click, then a hollow thud, and Reverie's eyes are as bright as stars. Without even looking inside, she pulls out a tattered bit of parchment and waves it in the air.

It's a map. A map of the hills, with a very specific point marked, and some notes at the bottom.

Wren whistles. "Damn."

"Well," Lark says, licking their lips. "That certainly looks tangible."

Reverie rolls her eyes and puts on an eerily accurate imitation of Lark's refined Izirm accent. Trust the Qelandian girl with a Federation accent to have extra tricks up her sleeve.

"Well done Reverie, marvelous work—"

"I don't speak like that," Lark interrupts, and Wren has to smother a grin at how they seem to be trying to look annoyed and are failing miserably.

"—you are obviously a woman of excellent skirt and character—"

Lark snatches the paper while Reverie devolves into giggles. "If only I could speak to your priorities. What kind of person lists their skirt ahead of their character?"

Reverie, getting to her feet, leans over the desk to rest on her elbows. This does fascinating things to the skirt in question, and on any other day, Wren might have taken this moment to appreciate it. Not, however, today.

Lark unfolds the map with a needlessly dramatic flourish, as if to tell Reverie to go fuck herself. Then, with a cough, they begin to study it.

Reverie flashes a grin at Wren, like a cat who got the cream.

"Alright then," Lark says a few moments later. "We'll set out in the morning. Should only be a few hours walk."

"Not now?" Wren asks, not because she *wants* to go now but because she had expected more urgency from them.

"Going after Nightingale with no rest and you injured is a recipe for disaster," Lark says, closing the map and tucking it into one of their pockets. "I'll be able to heal you more in the morning. Besides, Norak said something about a thank you. I think they're planning a party, but they said something about waiting on three of the teenagers to get back."

"Oh gods," Wren says, feeling awful that she had forgotten about them. "Has there been any word?"

"Not when we left, but we can go and find out," Lark says, tilting their head when they see Wren's concern. "Where did they go?"

"To get back the town gold from the... camp," Wren says, trailing off as too many pessimistic scenarios play out in her mind. "The retreat, they would have needed to hide—"

"I'm sure they knew that," Reverie says.

"Yeah." Wren swallows and wishes she believed her own words. "Yeah."

"Let's go and find them, then, so that we can have that party. We've had two days of nearly dying in two totally different ways," Reverie says. "We've earned it."

"Sure, let's go," Wren says, and Lark hurries to help her to her feet. "Oh! Did your spell work? Did it help?"

Reverie clasps her hands in front of her and beams. "Yeah! Had three of them standing there, dazed as anything, staring at the ground like it was a painting and not chalk. Charms are so fun."

It sounds faintly terrifying, the idea that such a spell could render one so gormless, but that's the great thing about having a Disciplined mage on *their* side. Wren wishes she had been able to see it.

"It bought Norak time to get to Lark, get patched up, and get back on the barricade so no more could get through," Reverie continues. "Couldn't ask for better than that."

"Exactly! Marvelous piece of work indeed." Lark smiles at Reverie. "Alright. Let's find these teenagers."

Chapter 12

The teenagers, it turns out, do not require finding.

There is a hollering in the streets, a joyous whooping that the three travellers follow until they come into the main street and see the three youths carrying a large wooden chest with exhausted and beaming smiles.

"You did it!" Wren exclaims. It is not quite surprise, not quite relief, but simply elation.

The world seems to right itself, as these three come home victorious and discard some of her greatest fears.

"We did it," one of the girls echoes, looking at her companions, who grin back.

"Yes, you did," says Norak from behind them.

He watches them with the pride of a big brother, and when he looks to Wren the relief for their safety is washed over his face.

"Now, it is done," he says, and Wren nods.

The town hall releases a breath when the teens enter with the chest. The bounty hits the ground, unimportant for a few moments, as the teens' families embrace them, congratulate them, and chastise them.

The room erupts into movement. One side is lined with beds or makeshift cots while the rest has been cleared to accommodate four bodies laid out with great care. Their hands are crossed and hold a simple daisy each. Three warriors, two middle aged and one in their prime. One old woman, with crackled spectacles arranged carefully on her face.

Lark finds a quiet moment to kneel by the librarian and look her over. They nod to themself and return to Wren and Reverie with haste.

"Were we right?" Wren asks.

"The slashes are congruent with Nightingale's quill blade."

"So she was here." Wren lets out a long breath. "Shit."

"A day ahead of us, because of us getting brought to the Collection on the way," Lark says with a nod.

"And she's after whatever is at the heart of that labyrinth."

"So we'll find her."

The wake for the fallen is almost ready to begin. One of the injured, a woman given so much deference by Norak that Wren is sure she must be the head guard, has her makeshift cot moved so that she can speak to the crowd.

Wren should be listening. But her memories pull her far away, back to her own town, hearing the voice of the mayor speak on those they had lost. Two guards. Loren and Taffy, best friends who had filled her home with laughter every day. A farmer, Paisley, who had tried to fight the bandits after they had scared his cows. A butcher named Fen who had always given their offcuts to house pets around the town. On that day, Wren had been one of the injured listening from the side, although the wake had been in the town square, not the hall. The stars had shone down on the victims of the raid, and Wren had been unable to wash the taste of defeat and grief from her mouth. She had not paid the due amount of attention at that wake either. Her mind had been racing, playing the memory of the cufflink in the mud over and over and putting together the pieces. Feeling nauseous. Feeling guilt for not hearing the eulogies of those she would miss.

It is a thing she could not admit, or say, but Wren is not one for lingering on the past. It serves only as a compass. It used to tell her to stay still, speaking nothing of going anywhere in particular. But the attack on home had kicked it into motion, pointing her to her uncles, to the truth, to justice.

Wren did not know these people, and her remembering them does not matter. What does matter, is if she can prevent deaths like theirs, if she can bring their killers to justice. That is what they would care about, so that is what she'll do. So long as she can determine what her brand of justice actually is.

As the speeches come to an end, the drinks are poured, wine and ale in good measure. Stories flow just as freely, and it feels right to stay at the back of the room and sip wine.

Lark is flitting around the room doing gods only know what, while Reverie is sitting on her crate and strumming at her lyre, a wordless song of soft beauty and melancholy. It's perfect, and Wren gives her a nod of approval when Reverie catches her eye from across the room.

The despair that had been hanging in the air of Hanos is gone. Now, grief and hope in equal measure have replaced it, and it is bittersweet and potent on Wren's tongue. The wine tastes dull in comparison.

Reverie transitions into a song about a friend who leaves on a long journey, with the one who stays reminiscing about seeing them again one day. By the time she hits the chorus, there are no dry eyes left in the room, even on the people who had been holding it together.

Wren supposes anyone can sing a sad song, but if Wren didn't know it already she would have sworn Reverie were the songwriter by how much emotion twists the notes as she sings the part of the friend left behind.

It evokes visions of Reverie on a merchant caravan travelling from place to place, charming all she encounters with such songs, living off tips from adoring fans.

She has magic that can make warriors fall. Family armour, family expectations, a quest for a sword. And yet, for all of Reverie's assurances of those things, seeing her sing now has it all ring hollow.

Here she is, giving a new definition to Wren's understanding of music and what it can do. Here she is, somewhere not at all where she ought to be, and exactly in the right place at the right time.

Wren can at least be grateful for that. She listens to the sad song, and the one that comes after, and lets herself be lost to the ballads of tragedy.

During the third song, a voice from near Wren makes her start and whip around.

"Thank you!"

Wren turns to see one of the civilian archers, a dark haired girl not quite an adult but plenty limber enough to defend her town. Her eyes are bright, shining with something powerful enough to make Wren's stomach turn.

"Oh," Wren says, eloquently. "You're—you're welcome."

"He's saying you got the leader, the ice mage," the girl gushes. "That's why they retreated."

"Who's *he*?" Wren asks with bewilderment.

"That boy over there." A point of a finger reveals a child of about seven now talking animatedly with Reverie, who has paused her singing to scribble into a notebook with furious abandon. "Apparently he was watching through the window, because he'd been following the guy for a while."

"What was a child doing—" Wren cuts herself off with a shake of her head. "Well. Yeah. I did. I'm just glad it worked."

"Me too," the girl says. "Thank you. We won't ever forget what you did."

Envy, that ugly thing that has barely touched her before today, seizes Wren's chest once again. Envy of this girl, of all of her peers, that they had received the rescuer she would have given anything for. And then, almost as quickly as it had arrived, it is shoved out of place by guilt. Guilt not about to give up its home.

Wren could have killed him and ensured no one else suffered by his hand. She could have called the retreat herself by dumping his body on the barricade, but even thinking of it fills her with revulsion.

How can she feel so awful for doing too little but not be able to stomach doing just enough? What is too much?

"Are you okay?" the girl asks, eyes wide.

"Just tired, and hurt," Wren says, half honestly.

"Right. I'll just—thank you, again."

The girl hurries off, and Wren can only sigh with relief. She gets a few minutes of peace to drink her wine before Lark appears at her side.

"Where have you been?" Wren asks them.

"Corroborating," Lark replies, as if that explains anything at all. They help themself to a glass of wine.

"Corroborating?"

"The map we found, it has a bit at the bottom. Cryptic, poem sort of thing. It warns about the trials inside the labyrinth."

"Trials?"

Lark shrugs and takes a sip of their wine. "I've been picking the brains of a few locals, seeing if they know anything else. Local rumour, you know. Valuable thing."

"And?"

"Skill *and* character. That's, apparently, what the trials test. One of them was sure it wasn't something a single person could pass, because no one is so skilled or unflawed."

There is an odd smile on their lips, even more odd when paired with the nervous tap of their fingers against their arm.

"Why is that good?" Wren asks.

"Oh, it might be terrible," Lark says. "Nightingale is awfully skilled. But I can't say I'm not... tickled, at the prospect of her having to prove her character. We might catch up to her."

"We'd better," Wren says, but then she has to snort at the image of Nightingale, the callous and whimsical terror, standing in front of some mighty being trying to convince them she is of decent moral standing.

Lark laughs too, but the tension in their body betrays the difficulty of the topic. Wren has even more empathy for their situation now. She wants to ask if they have a plan, anything in that funny head of theirs which will mean they don't face the same defeat as their last encounter with Nightingale. But perhaps, until she has a plan to stop her uncles, that would be hypocrisy yet again. Perhaps, just for a moment, they can feel this strange pain together, and be.

She moves her wine glass into her left hand so that she can put her right one on of their arms and give it a squeeze. Lark glances at her, startled.

"We'll be okay," is all Wren says, and something powerful escapes Lark's body in a long exhale. Some weight, some anxiety, for now eased a little.

"Yes," Lark says, almost sounding as if they believe her. "Of course we will."

A long strum of a lyre calls their attention to the centre of the room. Reverie looks out through the townsfolk and gives them a smile.

"I have now, the story of the hour," Reverie says. "Be gracious, it's a quick composition. But it's for you. To remember."

Then, she begins to sing. It's middling speed and heartfelt, words immediately hitting hard.

Fire and ice, too much too fast
We knew we could not last
We had to make our stand
Arrow to arrow, hand to hand

There is a murmur through the crowd, one of recognition and fascination.

We needed one to turn the tide
To hold strong, and fight for what's right
And she came, flowers and swo-ord
Just what we were praying fo-or

She found the one behind it all
Steel meets ice, all for all
But good will win over greed
Her strength brought him to his kne-es

Sound the retreat, or meet your end
There's no more luck and blood to spend
With one last glance he turned and fled
And with that home was safe again

Her final strum echoes and the townsfolk erupt into applause. Reverie beams, and bows her head in recognition.

"The Hero of Hanos," someone shouts. "Here's to her!"

Glasses are raised, and Wren had already felt like she'd been smacked over the head with a blunt instrument but now it is so much worse as dozens of eyes turn to her. How does one even form thoughts? It's surreal in a way that neither delights nor horrifies.

They toast her, and she nods because there is nothing else to do, and then everything is calm as they demand Reverie play The Hero of Hanos again. All calm, but for Wren's alarmed heart.

She glances at Lark.

"Did she *just* write that?" they ask as soon as she does so. "Remarkable. Don't tell her I said that." They quirk an eyebrow. "Ever think you'd have your own song?"

"No, I didn't," Wren says, unable to help how her eyes slip away from them and towards Reverie instead. She is too afraid of what Lark might say. It's not fair, but isn't actually fair that she should have to hold eye contact the whole time against her instinct and wishes to have a conversation. Absurd magical curse indeed.

Maybe one day, everything will be good and better and her brothers can laugh upon hearing a song written for her. Maybe she will laugh with them. Something will click. But today? Today it sits all wrong, like bad cheese in her stomach.

Better that she think of it as Reverie's achievement, a song for people who may need it.

Someone has found a lute and begun a new song, and Reverie is able to slip away to grab a drink. Once it's in her hand, she comes to see Wren and Lark.

"So?" she asks.

"You've got a gift," Wren says.

Reverie's eyes shine. "Yeah." She bites her lip. "So, you liked it?"

"They won't forget it," Wren says as honestly as she can. "It's an amazing tribute." *To their history. Not to me.*

Something crosses Reverie's face, too quick for Wren to make sense of, but it turns into a thoughtfulness that tilts her head.

"I am pretty amazing," she says a moment later.

"And your modesty, continuously astounding," Lark says from next to Wren, as soon as Reverie's eyes drift to them.

Reverie smiles and crosses her arms. "You can't tell me they didn't need a song like that."

"You're right. I can't."

The way Reverie preens at that reminds Wren of a cat, or stories about colourful birds from the elven kingdoms that parade their bright colours.

But then it fades, and Reverie casts her eyes about the room and for the first time that Wren has known her, looks totally lost.

"I've never—" Reverie bites her lip. "I've been to funerals, but this is different. I don't know what I should be doing."

"Nothing really," Wren says. "It's not about you. Or us. It's about them. What we can do is be here for them if they need us."

Reverie's face softens with gratitude. "I can do that," she says. "I can be whatever they need."

With that, she moves to sit with a group who are singing along to the musician.

"Let's get you into a chair," Lark says to Wren a few moments later. "You're doing an awful job of resting, you know."

They say it as if either of them have any skill with such things. As if they are capable of sitting still and idle without itching to go back out into the world.

"I learned from the best," Wren says, with a meaningful look, and Lark somehow manages to tut and grin in the same moment.

"Well, maybe one day you can teach me how to see what people need the way you do," Lark says. "Even Miss Rosetia seems to be hit and miss in that area."

"I don't know if it's that simple. You had a weird upbringing, and if she's from some adventuring family then she probably did too. I just... know people like this, because I grew up with them."

"No, you're good with everyone."

Wren laughs. "I'm really not."

"When you speak, people listen."

"I can never find the words that you do."

How strange it is, to hold Lark's gaze and see envy that matches her own, for them to be as different as possible and coveting what the other has. And meanwhile, Reverie has something else altogether.

"I guess we're a good team for a reason," Wren says, with a smile.

Lark smiles back. "That's very true."

They sit in the corner together, and the night goes on. Wren wonders how sitting in a corner with pain ebbing through her could be so pleasant, but it might have something to do with the firelight in Lark's eyes. Or the cadence of their voice, speaking on a thousand things and yet very little at all.

If so, she is simply going to be grateful and think no further on it.

Chapter 13

Reverie is absent from breakfast. Wren wonders if it is connected to the honking she had heard outside her window around dawn, or how upon coming downstairs she and Lark had discovered Ferdinand sat in a corner, plainly fuming.

He doesn't move from the spot as Lark and Wren help themselves to the simple porridge that is all that is on offer, and Wren gets the sense that the goose cannot move at all.

Karma is amusing like that. Wren ponders ways to mock him before deciding the best thing to do would be to give him no attention at all and to let him continue being bored.

As such, Lark and Wren eat porridge at a table in the otherwise empty tavern and discuss how Viken and Vasil could have become mages; which here means that Wren eats her porridge and Lark gives her an enthusiastic and informative lecture about the nature of innate magic.

"It's like baking a cake," Lark is saying. "The magical source is the last ingredient to make a mage, but you have no idea how long it's going to take to get a mage. If there's mystery ingredients, like latent magic in the bloodline, or environmental factors at the time of encountering the magical source... these things might make it faster or slower or you might never get a cake at all. There are too many possible factors, in this world, too much errant magic we either don't notice or simply can't quantify."

It's rather a lot to take in with spoons of porridge. Wren swallows her current mouthful and tries to wrap her head around it.

"But their cakes finished at the same time," she says. "The same day, Vasil said."

"Yes, which is fascinating because the only logical explanation is that they encountered exactly the same magical source at exactly the same time, and had such a lack of mystery ingredients that their magic had identical incubation periods."

"So first it's a cake, and now it's an egg," Wren tries to clarify.

"Yes," Lark says, before wincing. "Well, no, obviously it's *neither*—"

"Lark, I didn't actually think we were talking about cakes—"

"No, no, I know, the point is that your uncle is human and Vasil is part elven, you said? Usually I would expect that to make a difference, what with the old magic in elven bloodlines, but it didn't, so the magic must not have any roots in anything close to the fey."

"But if it was the same source, why did one get fire and the other get ice?" Wren asks.

Lark's hands gesture wildly and no sound at all comes out for several moments. Finally, they say, "I have absolutely no idea, and I'm not going to be able to stop thinking about it until I know. There *will* be a reason."

It's at this moment that Reverie twirls down the stairs, holding her breastplate armour awkwardly under her arm while she finishes tying up the laces of her knee high boots.

"Morning!" she chirps as she sits and begins to put her breastplate over her shirt. "Gods, I hate this fucking thing."

"Do you want a hand?" Wren asks.

Reverie's hands pause on the clasps. "No, I'm fine," she says a moment later, and she persists awkwardly. "So. Labyrinth?"

Lark all at once takes on a manner so serious that they stop humming and set down their spoon.

"Yes, I have a lot of thoughts on this," they say, which is Wren's cue to decide to multitask. She pulls her case of affirmation elixirs out to mix this week's dose. There's facial hair, body hair, voice, jawline, and several others. Her mixes only need miniscule adjustments each time if at all, and Wren knows the process by heart now. "Nightingale wants the power source. Your uncles want the power source, because someone else paid them to get it. If this is as powerful as the stories say, it could turn the tide of the war."

"Does Nightingale care about the war?" Wren asks as she drinks the potion that keeps her facial hair repressed. It tastes a bit like strawberries, and a bit like soap.

"I wouldn't think so," Lark says. "But she cares about her freedom, and someone helped her escape. Call me cynical, but I don't imagine they did so out of the goodness, or even the awfulness, of their hearts. More likely, they asked for something in return. *Or*, she's already deviated from anything she promised them and is out to get this for herself. Equally likely."

Reverie snorts. "Helpful."

"I can only work with the crumbs we have," Lark says. "She said it was just the beginning. The thing in the Collection said they were going to change the world as we know it. This thing in the Labyrinth might just enable someone to do that. The Wayfinder can sense connections we can't—it could all be the same person, pulling strings. Or it could be numerous individuals with separate designs on the war. Nightingale might be the only one who could tell us."

"But she won't, right?" Reverie guesses.

Lark sighs into their hand. "Well, no. Probably not. Not unless we have information worth trading."

"Or if we trick her."

Lark's eyes roll again and they shake their head. "She is not easily tricked."

"Maybe not by you, if you're her ex," Reverie says as if it's obvious. "But she's never met *me*."

"You're not tricky, you're flashy, there's a difference."

"Then how did I get away with killing my father?" Reverie asks.

The table goes silent. Reverie's gaze is steadfast, unwavering in the face of Lark's utter shock. Wren has so much whiplash she is stuck holding a tube of glittering potion to her mouth and has nothing to say at all.

"I—" Lark opens their mouth, closes it, and despite having Reverie's eyes locked on them, finds no words.

The moment shatters with the sound of Reverie's laughter.

"By the Winter Wolf's furry ass, I had you," she cackles. "*Not tricky, flashy, there's a difference.*"

Lark purses their lips. "Point made."

Wren, through all of this, can only rub her temples. "So... this might be some big conspiracy?"

"Or a power struggle between secretive factions," Lark says with agreement. "As if the council of bishops having a secret project isn't enough! A magical power source would certainly come in handy for whatever that is, I'd bet my other eye, but they would never ask individuals such as Nightingale or a roaming bandit captain to retrieve it."

"Maybe not officially," Wren says. "You know. As a group. But maybe one of them did. Maybe they're planning on lying about where they got it. Things are getting desperate."

"*That* seems more likely," Reverie says. "Never underestimate how one person can fuck everything up."

Lark's brows furrow. They do not argue, but the sigh they release is as heavy as a raincloud. "There are certainly people in several temples that might consider it a suitable means to an end, yes. The Trickster's temple, especially. Not that I actually know of anyone who isn't the High Bishop or the Deputy, and I'm not convinced that they're the real Deputy or High Bishop anyway given the nature of—" Lark coughs. "Well. You know."

Wren does, and Reverie nods as well. The Higher Pantheon is the dominant religion here in Qelandia too, so even someone as casually faithful as Wren knows worshippers of the Trickster rarely advertise their fealty, for a myriad of reasons. Wren can only assume it is infinitely more complicated within the

Theocracy of Izirm, where it is political as well as personal and spiritual.

"So, we have no idea who she's working for, and there's nothing we can trade this bitch," Reverie summarises.

"Well, it's not impossible, but it's not likely," Lark says. "It would have to be obscure enough that she hasn't come across it before, and interesting enough to be worth the trade. Do you have anything like that?"

Reverie glances at the goose who is still sitting in his banished corner, glowering at them all. Her gaze flicks back to Lark. "I wish."

"And I don't," Wren says. She begins packing away her affirmation elixirs.

"We'll work it out," Lark mutters, with the easy confidence that has fascinated Wren from the moment they met. "First stop: the labyrinth. If we can't reach her, the entire thing is pointless. We need to be wary of what we might fight in there. The map has a distinct warning." They pull out the bit of paper and begin to read. "The labyrinth is not prison but protection, beware all who enter. Only those with true virtue may use the Centre for just purposes. Trials are set, and will judge you."

Reverie grimaces. "Judge us? What does that mean?"

"Hard to say, but I'm sure that's far more of a Nightingale problem than one for us."

Wren gulps down the last of her morning coffee and puts the cup down on the table. "Alright. Are we going, then?"

They pack up, fetch Melora from where she had been staying outside the tavern since before the attack, and head for the guard house to bid Norak a final farewell. The young man is busy with several others, organising burial sites for the few dead and making plans for rebuilding priorities.

"Morning!" he says when he sees them. "Are you off, then?"

"We are." Lark offers a hand for him to shake, and gets a firm clasp. "Our own tricky business to sort out."

"Well, you always have friends here. We owe you."

"No, you don't," Lark insists, and Wren shakes her head as way of agreement with them.

"Good luck with everything," Reverie says to Norak. "You got this."

He smiles at her. "Yes, I think we do."

Wren moves in to shake Norak's hand as well. "Thanks. I—" *I needed to meet someone like you. I wish we could be friends. I wish I knew what to say.* "Look after yourself."

"Only so long as you take your own advice," he says, grinning. "Your life sounds more dangerous than mine."

She can't argue.

With that, they depart. The world grows quieter with each step away from the town, and once they reach the hill, Wren cannot resist looking back.

It's a mess, but it's going to recover. It is better for their help, for their intervention. That is a hard thing to ignore, and a belated smile comes to Wren's lips.

She will never stop helping those who need it. This whole business with the dragon war and the bishops and her uncle only shows that people with absurd power so rarely think of the regular people affected by their actions. Wren will not allow them to be forgotten, or go without someone in their corner.

"Wren! You good?" Reverie calls out.

Wren has fallen behind. She takes one more look at the town, then turns her eyes to the hills, and her friends, and the dangers beyond.

Good thing they have her to look after them.

TO BE CONTINUED

IN

VOLUME IV: THE LABYRINTH BECKONS

Afterword

Thanks so much for coming along for the next leg of the Catastrophe Incoming adventure. I hope Wren's POV was everything you were hoping it would be and more. If you've been waiting for Nightingale to return, don't worry, she really is back for Volume IV and in a big way!

If you enjoyed this book and the ones before it, I would be really grateful if you would consider leaving me a review on Goodreads and Amazon, as it really helps me out as an indie author.

If you'd like to read more from me, you can get a FREE BOOK, a fantasy mystery novelette called *The Curious Matter of Myron Manor,* if you sign up to my newsletter! Head to www.aimeedonnellan.com/newsletter or you can scan the QR code over the page.

If you'd like to find me on social media, you can find me on Twitter / X as @bardqueenaimee.

Everywhere else I am @aimeedonnellanwrites!

Acknowledgements

I'll keep these short and sweet. I am forever grateful to have the community that I do, cheering me on and helping me every step of the way. It was a delight to realise how many beta and ARC readers were frothing at the mouth for Wren's POV, and it's been a joy to see people connecting with her journey.

To my wonderful betas for this book, I owe you everything. Ceilidh, thank you for always being the hype person I need in my life. Norah, thanks so much for coming on board the beta team. Bryanna, you helped the themes of the book soar and come through clear. Senka, your gift for spotting word repetition is unparalleled and your nitpicking improves my work *so* much!

To my ARC readers: Nico, Cait, Keanna, and Lillian (your review made me wanna sob, actually). I'm so lucky to have you!

Kate, not only do you make me laugh with comments like "pog line" and "strength score of 8 max" (and you're right about the latter for Lark and Reverie, for sure), your gorgeous art never fails to make the covers shine and I am so grateful to have you as a part of this project.

Ty, thanks for always making sure the story and world make sure after I get carried away with a grand idea. Continuity editing rights for life.

Here's to the rest of the adventure. I can't wait to share it with you all.

The adventure continues in
VOLUME IV: THE LABYRINTH BECKONS

Turn the page for a special preview!

As the trio step inside, the sunlight is quickly drowned in the depths of the cavernous space. It extends before them, into the dark, until lanterns spark with bright green flames on the wall on either side of them.

The walls are covered with artwork, intricate designs that tell a story of the research and creation of a great power—something that, if the depictions are in any way accurate, amplifies the magical abilities of anyone that wields it.

"Oh, so *that's* what this thing does," Lark says. "What fascinating possibilities. No wonder powerful people with grand plans for the war are probably trying to get their hands on this." They simply will not think about exactly which people those might be, lest the possible answers be too awful to contemplate for long.

"How old is all this?" asks an awed Wren.

"At least six hundred years old," Lark says. "Incredible, isn't it? If we'd never been to that town, we'd have never known this was here. There should have been *some* reference to it in the Scholar's archive, but I've been over every inch of their magical artifacts section, I'd have definitely remembered coming across records of anything like this, and if Nightingale and *I* couldn't find it, then—"

"What if *she* found it?" Wren asks. "And hid it from you?"

The pair of questions nearly stop Lark in their tracks. They want to argue that it couldn't be true. But Nightingale feigning ignorance around a magical artifact in a ruin is *exactly* how they had ended up here. Cursed, torn apart, seeing things in the world no one else can. Even if that particular untruth had been before the murders had started, this would simply be another in a growing collection of lies.

They meet Wren's eyes, let out a soft sigh, and choose to let the defeat of it speak for itself.